P9-CCB-051

THERE IN **THE COURTYARD** OF THE INN THE SHEPHERDS FOUND THE INFANT JESUS

THE ILLUSTRATED
BIBLE
STORY BOOK
NEW TESTAMENT

Stories retold for children by
SEYMOUR LOVELAND

With an Introduction by
KATHARINE LEE BATES

Illustrated by
MILO WINTER

DOVER PUBLICATIONS, INC.
MINEOLA, NEW YORK

Planet Friendly Publishing
✔ Made in the United States
✔ Printed on Recycled Paper
GREEN EDITION   Learn more at www.greenedition.org

At Dover Publications we're committed to producing books in an earth-friendly manner and to helping our customers make greener choices.

Manufacturing books in the United States ensures compliance with strict environmental laws and eliminates the need for international freight shipping, a major contributor to global air pollution.

And printing on recycled paper helps minimize our consumption of trees, water and fossil fuels. The text of *The Illustrated Bible Story Book—New Testament* was printed on paper made with 10% post-consumer waste, and the cover was printed on paper made with 10% post-consumer waste. According to Environmental Defense's Paper Calculator, by using this innovative paper instead of conventional papers, we achieved the following environmental benefits:

**Trees Saved: 12 • Air Emissions Eliminated: 1,017 pounds
Water Saved: 4,184 gallons • Solid Waste Eliminated: 542 pounds**

For more information on our environmental practices, please visit us online at www.doverpublications.com/green

Copyright

Copyright © 1925 by Rand McNally & Company. Reproduced with permission.
CD content copyright © 2008 by Dover Publications, Inc.
All rights reserved.

Bibliographical Note

The Illustrated Bible Story Book—New Testament, first published by Dover Publications, Inc., in 2008, is reproduced from the work first published by Rand McNally & Company, Chicago and New York, in 1925. This edition includes a new audio recording to accompany the text.

International Standard Book Number
ISBN-13: 978-0-486-46835-8
ISBN-10: 0-486-46835-6

Audio recording produced by Blane & DeRosa Productions, Inc.

Manufactured in the United States of America
Dover Publications, Inc., 31 East 2nd Street, Mineola, N.Y. 11501

THE ILLUSTRATED
BIBLE
STORY BOOK
NEW TESTAMENT

THE INTRODUCTION

THE life of Jesus Christ, related with supreme dignity and surpassing beauty in the gospels, cannot be told too often. In this book of New Testament stories the life of Christ is set forth in simple language for young children. The four gospels tell mainly about the manhood of Jesus: how He journeyed from place to place with His little group of disciples, healing the sick, preaching the Word of God. Jesus was Himself the Word, for God is Love and the life of Christ was Love. I wish that we might have had one gospel more, written by Mary, to tell us of the clinging child, the eager boy, the earnest youth who was the light of the carpenter's home in Nazareth. The longing to know more of those early years has been so great that simple people, centuries ago, caught at floating legends that we no longer credit: how Jesus, at play with other children, molding clay into images of donkeys and cows and dogs, fashioned little sparrows that flew at his command; how when old Joseph, who, the story said, "was not very skilful at his carpenter's trade," would find he had made a door too wide or a shelf too long, Jesus would touch the timber and instantly door or shelf "became as Joseph would have it"; how one day Jesus' playfellows "spread their garments on the ground for Him to sit on, and having made a crown of flowers, put it upon His head and stood on His right and left as the guards of a king. And if anyone happened to pass by, they took him by force and said, 'Come hither, and worship the King, that you may have a prosperous journey.'"

Though these tales are only the fancies of wistful hearts, not the memories of those who had seen that blessed childhood, yet even in these there is at least a grain of truth. We know from what Jesus said and did that He cared for all living creatures and especially for birds; we are sure that His young hands always were quick to help, and we can easily understand that the little Nazarenes would make Him the center of their games. Devout old painters liked to picture the carpenter's shop: Joseph busy with his saw and Mary sitting by, her sewing fallen to her knee while her look dwelt tenderly on the Holy Child as He gathered up the chips and shavings, with a flutter-winged cluster of cherubs doing their best to aid.

Is there any surer way to make the boyhood of Jesus more real and vivid to us? Yes, from pictures and books about the Holy Land and from visiting these scenes of Jesus' youth, we can see something of what He saw; from brief mentions in the New Testament we can learn a little of the family life; and from Christ's own references to features of the landscape and the happenings of the neighborhood so familiar to Him, we can glean yet more. So together let us in imagination go, as pilgrims for hundreds and hundreds of years have gone, by sea, by land, in dream, in prayer, to Nazareth.

Palestine is in size but a small strip of the earth. An express train could run through it from top to bottom in three hours. It consists, from west to east of a coast lying beside the blue Mediterranean, a low coast broken only by the long, level lift of Mount Carmel; then of a range of hills running north and south, on one of whose slopes Nazareth is built; then of the Jordan valley widening out into the Sea of Galilee; and, finally, a bordering table-land. The four divisions, in the time of Christ, were Galilee to the north, then Samaria in the center, farthest to the south, Judea, and Perea which included all the region lying east of the Jordan and south of the Jabbok.

Nazareth is now a large town, as Syrian towns go, sweeping well up the hillside, its white, flat-roofed houses gleaming out from fig trees and olive groves. Under Roman rule it probably was even larger, an important "city," as the New Testament always terms it, among two hundred towns and villages of Galilee where people lived in such close quarters that Jesus may early have learned to slip away into the hills for quiet thought. The house was probably built of stone, as the houses of Nazareth are today, and may have had, like some of these, a garden inclosed by a cactus hedge. Joseph almost certainly was a mason as well as a carpenter, for the builders of his time worked in stone more than in wood. Perhaps his son was taught to carve in marble. One likes to think that Jesus, as a boy, may have known the joy of the artist. At every hour He knew the thrill of beauty, and often would have climbed "unto the brow of the hill whereon their city was built" for the wonderful view reaching from the purples of Mount Carmel to the dazzling snows of Mount Hermon.

If Joseph had his workshop at home, his house, its square outlines softened by blossoming vines like the close-pressing houses of his neighbors, may possibly have had two stories. A Jew of a proud old family descended from King David, Joseph was by no means ashamed of being a workingman, for the Hebrew commanded that every boy be taught a trade. As one of their rabbis wrote: "Labor honors the laborer." On a summer morning, the little household would be early astir. On the flat roof, whose low parapet guarded a restless child from a fall, Jesus would have been sleeping snugly wrapt in a gay-colored quilted coverlet, not unlike our "puffs" or "comforters." From the open housetop, before His eyes had closed in a tired boy's sound slumber, Jesus would have seen the same moon and stars, the same trooping constellations, that keep watch over us today, and on waking He would have looked on the fresh rose of dawn, lifting His heart to the joy of a new day. He would have been happy in the color and fragrance of the hour and would have had a gentle smile for the doves resting on the parapet, unafraid as He stepped near.

Then quite naturally Jesus would have risen, taken up his light bed and carried it down the ladder-stair to the large living-room below. Here the family quilts were each neatly rolled up and tucked away on a low bench that ran against the walls nearly all the way around the room. On this ledge were arranged such few articles as even the simplest housekeeping needs — clay pots and bowls and a lamp shaped like a saucer with the wick floating on the surface of the olive oil. On either side of the door stood a tall, slim water jar. In a corner of the room was a great wooden chest, painted in some bright design, holding the family treasures — scrolls of the Law and the Prophets, finely woven robes and other choice raiment.

In another corner of the room might be seen a broad stool, colored as gaily as the chest, and here and there were great clay vessels for the storing of grain and vegetables, wicker baskets of fruit, and a pile of palm-leaf mats, which, spread upon the floor or upon the bench, gave the parents easier couches. Jesus, indeed, liked best of all, when the night was warm, to sleep out on the hills, rolled in his loose Galilean coat.

By the time the washing and prayers, required by the Jewish rule, were finished, and Joseph had come in from his workshop — or come up, if the living-room formed a second floor — Mary was placing on the painted stool, now drawn out into the open space, a tray bearing thin rounds of new bread and a large bowl of rice, into which Joseph and any guests, sitting on their heels in eastern fashion, around the low stool, dipped their hands in turn. For Mary had risen first of all the household and, one of the red water jars gracefully balanced on her erect head, had tripped down the stony road to the town spring — now called Lady Mary's Fountain — for water. Perhaps, too, she, with the help of a neighbor, another Mother in Israel, had been grinding corn at her hand-mill, lightly kneading the moistened meal, and then baking the dough, spread into these thin layers, in the neighborhood oven.

Breakfast over, water would be brought for the washing of fingers, and Joseph would give his son the task for the day. If he bade Jesus help him in the shop, we may be sure that many a passer-by lingered in the open door to hear the strange, wise talk of the bright-faced young apprentice sitting on the floor and working away with plane or drill on the flat board that served as carpenter's bench. But if it were a holiday, how gladly Jesus went out on one of His long rambles! He could walk to Mount Tabor in two hours, to the Sea of Galilee in five. And all the way He was noting where the foxes had their holes and the birds of the air their nests, delighting in the scarlet splendor of the wild lilies — "even Solomon in all his glory was not arrayed like one of these" — watching the life of

9

vineyard and threshing floor and market place. He would meet shepherds leading their flocks through green pastures, gathering the lambs in their arms and carrying them in their bosom. He would pause to hear the pipers, on the road to some grand wedding, playing a tune for the dancing children who frolicked after them. He would follow the bees to find where they hid their honeycomb. He would stand to see the sower scattering his seed, a fisherman letting down his net, a hen gathering her chickens under her wings. And all these common things had deep and beautiful meaning for Him, the more common the more divine, as if His Father in Heaven were, through them, giving Him a message. Mary often felt that she did not understand when her star-eyed son told her of the thoughts that had come to Him from the fields and hills, "but His mother kept all these sayings in her heart. And Jesus increased in wisdom and stature, and in favor with God and man."

KATHARINE LEE BATES

THE CONTENTS

THE COMING OF THE KING

STANDING NEAR THE TEMPLE ALTAR, ZACHARIAS SAW THE ANGEL GABRIEL

BIBLE STORY BOOK

A WONDERFUL MESSAGE

It was a beautiful evening. The sun had put on his scarlet robe and was all ready to say good night to the world. His rays, like long, slender fingers, reached out over the sky as though flinging a farewell to all the little folks before he slipped so far out of sight that no one could find him until morning. Up in the blue heavens one brave little star twinkled merrily. Perhaps if stars could speak we might have heard this one say, "Cheer up, children, I'm going to be with you until the sun comes back."

What do you suppose the star saw as it flashed and sparkled? A beautiful church on top of a high hill in a beautiful city. This church was called the Temple, and the city was Jerusalem. Everything was so lovely that if you had walked through the great silver and gold gates and into the temple courts, you might have thought you were in fairyland. One of those big gates was so large and heavy that it would have taken forty children, all pushing at once, to open it. This great brass gate must have dazzled the people's eyes when the sun shone on it. They called it the Beautiful Gate.

The people who belonged to this church did not want everybody to come inside of it, so they built two strong stone walls around it. Inside these walls, but outside the church itself, most of the people prayed. Zacharias, the priest, went inside of the church because he had something very important to do there. At twilight, just as the first star peeped out of the blue sky, he must throw some sweet-smelling powders, called incense, on the hot coals that burned on the golden altar. This was the silent time when nobody, not even a chatterbox child, made a noise. Everyone was praying with his heart instead of with his lips.

What a smoke the incense did make! Zacharias waited until it cleared away. Then how he must have rubbed his eyes in surprise, and stared at the golden altar! He was sure no one had been near the altar when he threw on the incense! But now some one was beside it. He had heard no one come in. How could the visitor have come there? Zacharias was sure his visitor was an angel. Only a messenger of God could come in so quietly and look so kindly. When Zacharias saw the angel in the temple he must have been frightened, for when Gabriel spoke he told him he need have no fear and said, "I bring you good news."

SILENTLY ZACHARIAS MOTIONED TO THE WAITING PEOPLE TO GO HOME

Of course Zacharias should have known that Gabriel brought happy tidings. This angel never brought anything but good news to people. There was one thing the old priest and his wife wanted more than anything else in the world, and that was a little child of their own. The message Gabriel brought Zacharias and his wife Elizabeth, was this: "You shall have a son and his name shall be John." But Gabriel told Zacharias even more than this. The little John was to be a wonderful child. He was to make many people happy. When he grew to be a man he was to tell the people to get ready for the King, for now their real King was coming.

You remember how the Hebrews asked Samuel to make Saul their king, and what a very poor king Saul was. Since then the Hebrews had had a great many kings, but only three of them had been good ones. Now they were watching for the perfect King that God had promised to send them. Gabriel told Zacharias that the King would soon be here.

When we are going to have guests we get ready for them. What a task Mother has cleaning the rooms, dusting and straightening the furniture, and cooking good things for the company to eat! John, the little boy

THROUGH THE BEAUTIFUL GATE WALKED ZACHARIAS

he motioned to the waiting people to go home. Then slowly he walked through the Beautiful Gate and down to his own small house. Can't you see these two old people, Elizabeth and Zacharias, as they sat close beside each other? The lamplight shone on Elizabeth's white hair while she watched what her husband wrote on a tablet. He was writing the wonderful message Gabriel had brought him. He could not speak, for not since the angel's visit had Zacharias been able to say a word. But I know that he was happy, for Gabriel had said his promised son was to be the herald who should announce the coming of the King.

who was coming to Zacharias and Elizabeth, when he had grown to be a man was going to tell the people to get ready for the expected King. He was not going to tell them to build a great palace for him. John was coming before the King came so that he could tell everybody to prepare for him. He was going to tell the people to make their hearts ready to love the King when He came. That is a much better way to get ready for company than dusting rooms, cleaning furniture, and preparing food.

Out of the church and into the outer court went Zacharias. Silently

ZACHARIAS WRITING GABRIEL'S WONDERFUL MESSAGE
ON A TABLET FOR ELIZABETH

MARY

The Hebrews wanted a good king. One like David would have suited them best. Bad kings had ruined them. The poor people worked hard but each year grew poorer and poorer, because the kings took away from them almost everything they had, to make their own palaces richer and more beautiful.

In the Oriental country where the Hebrews lived, no one cared for the poor or those who were ill. If you had walked through a street in one of the cities in this land when Jesus lived there, you would have seen many things that would have made you sorry.

Homeless sick people staggered along the road until they could go no farther. Then they dropped by the roadside and lay in the dust until they died. The blind and the crippled sat beside the road begging. Perhaps there would be whole days when they had nothing to eat. You would be very likely to see a small girl or boy in the street snatching a bone from a half-starved dog, each trying to get a bit of food a rich neighbor had thrown away.

In all the land there were no doctors and no nurses for little sick babies. There were no hospitals and no clean white beds. Weary, sad-looking mothers held their suffering children in their arms while they begged for something to eat. But no one paid any attention. In that country no one loved the unhappy and hungry people. They had been forgotten.

There were other people in this country who were not rich, but who had homes and enough to eat. Some of these people were sure God would remember them. And He did. He had promised to send them a King. This one would be different from any king they had ever had. He would love every one of them. He would make well all those who were ill. He would make the wicked wish to be good, and the unhappy people glad.

BLIND AND CRIPPLED BEGGARS SAT BY THE WAYSIDE

MARY FEEDING THE DOVES IN THE COURTYARD

When God speaks, people cannot hear Him unless they are ready to listen. Zacharias, the priest, had been ready, and so he had seen and heard Gabriel, God's messenger. In all the land of the Hebrews there was only one other person who was ready to listen to a messenger from God. Who do you suppose that person was? Anyone in Nazareth could have told you. It was a humble Jewish maiden named Mary.

You will want to know how Mary looked, I am sure. We shall have to guess. Now shut your eyes and let us make a picture of Mary for ourselves. I'm sure you can see her.

Think of the sweetest and dearest face you ever saw. A face whose smile always made your heart glad. Such a face must have been like Mary's. A happy little maid who could talk with God's angel, Gabriel, must have had a sweet face, always cheery and full of sunshine. I am sure everyone who looked at her felt happier. When she talked or sang, even the singing of the birds did not sound sweeter. We can be sure that Mary had a kind heart, gentle, winning ways, a helpful spirit and loved everybody. God's angels do not bring good news to disagreeable people.

THE ANGEL GABRIEL BRINGS GOD'S WONDERFUL
MESSAGE TO MARY

one thing we can be certain; when he came he found Mary busy. God never calls lazy people. He gives his tasks only to those who are willing to work.

Into the court of Mary's house came Gabriel. "Hail, thou that art highly favored, the Lord is with thee. Blessed art thou among women," was his greeting.

Mary looked up at him in astonishment. Did the stranger think she was a princess? Such a greeting was given only to the rich and powerful. And Mary was neither. What could this beautiful stranger mean?

Then Gabriel spoke again. "The King is coming. He will soon be here. You have found favor with God, and a little child who is to be the great King will be given to you."

Into Mary's heart there came a great gladness. She was to be the mother of the promised King. Through her, God would remember and bless His people. The child that He was going to place in her arms would love all people and help them in all their troubles. Do you wonder that she sang with joy, "Henceforth all generations shall call me blessed"! She had prayed for her people and God had heard. Her son Jesus would save His people because He was also the Son of God.

Mary must often have felt sorry for those who were ill and poor. I am certain that many a tiny sick baby felt better because Mary had cared for it. When she prayed, I know she asked God to hurry and send the promised King. Many people besides Mary were praying for the coming of the great King. Mary really believed that God heard her prayer and would answer. But I fear the other people said in their hearts, "We will pray about it, but God will not hear us." And of course God did not hear that kind of prayer.

We do not know whether it was in the evening or in the morning that Gabriel visited Mary. But of

THE STORY THE STAR TOLD

What do we see at night that we cannot see in the daytime? The stars, of course. How black the nights would be without our friends, the stars! When I was little I liked to think that the stars were little people with dresses of different colors. Some stars wear pretty yellow dresses, others white or blue, and still others red or green.

One night a star twinkled and beckoned as if it wanted to speak to me. I thought it wished to tell me a story.

The story I think the star wanted to tell me that night is a beautiful story. I'm sure the little star knew all about it because when all the wonderful things in the story happened the star was dancing and twinkling in the sky just as it was that night I thought it wanted to tell it to me. And this is the story it told:

"One evening, long, long ago, the stars were all shining brightly. They were trying their best to give light to a few shepherds who were keeping night watches over their sheep on a hillside in a far-away country. If the stars had not shone so brightly a hungry wolf might have come and carried off a sheep or a lamb. Suddenly a shepherd on

WHEN THE SHEPHERDS LOOKED UP RIGHT BESIDE THEM
THEY SAW AN ANGEL IN SHINING GARMENTS

watch was sure he heard music. He looked up at the stars and called to his companions to come and watch them. They glowed and sparkled as though they were alive with happiness. They were trying to tell the shepherds that the angel of the Lord was coming to them with some wonderful news.

"And sure enough, when the shepherds looked up, there they saw, in shining garments, the angel standing right beside them. His face shone with such a wonderful light it made everything on the hillside glow. At first the shepherds were frightened. But the angel looked so kind and when he spoke to them

21

his voice rang out so clear and so sweet that they all knew he came bringing them good news. Then the watching shepherds crowded close to the angel to hear the story he had to tell them.

"'To-night,' the angel said unto them, 'is the most wonderful night since the world was made. For there is born to you in Bethlehem this day, a little Child a Savior who is Christ the Lord.'

"Then the music the shepherds heard grew louder and clearer. It was a song, and a great company of angels was singing it. There were so many of them the shepherds could not count them. This was the song

AS THE SHEPHERDS JOURNEYED HOMEWARD THEY
SANG THE SONG THE ANGELS SANG

the angels sang as they floated away toward the stars:

'Glory to God in the highest, and on earth peace good will toward men.'

"After the light had faded and the song had ended, the shepherds did not wait a moment. They were in a hurry to get to Bethlehem and see the little Christ Child. Off they started on their journey. In their haste they may have run all the way.

"The courtyard of the inn was crowded with people. Tired children were sleeping on the stone floor. Sleepy donkeys and camels nodded and blinked at the shepherds. How

TIRED CHILDREN WERE SLEEPING ON THE FLOOR AND
SLEEPY DONKEYS AND CAMELS WERE NODDING

could the shepherds hope to find a tiny baby in the midst of such a great crowd? But the angel had told the shepherds that the little Christ Child was here, and of course they would find him. And so they did. Lying on some straw in a manger, an inclosed place in the courtyard of the inn, was the little child Jesus. His mother and father were with him.

"The shepherds stood very still as they looked down upon the tiny baby. Perhaps they were listening again to the angels' song. Then one by one they tiptoed quietly out of the courtyard. And as they went slowly back to the green hillside far-away, they sang the song they had heard the angels sing."

Then the little star hid itself behind a fleecy cloud and I knew the story was ended. But soon a single bright beam, like a long slender finger, gleamed through the cloud, and then a starry face appeared. "O little star," I said, "I have heard that story before. It is in the Bible." Then the star twinkled and danced as though it were laughing at me.

"I, too, have heard all the Bible stories," said the little star. "And I have seen them all, for I have been in the sky ever since the world was made."

THE STAR
AND THE MAGI

Years and years ago, when people had no clocks to tell them the time and no maps to guide them when they traveled, they watched the stars. These twinkling little friends in the sky never made a mistake in the time and always knew exactly where they were going. "We will follow the stars," the people said when starting on a journey, and the friendly stars always showed them the way they should go.

Some Wise Men in the East, called the Magi, spent every night watching the stars. Their big, wise books—scrolls—had told them that a

THEIR SCROLLS TOLD THE MAGI OF A BRIGHT NEW STAR

THE MAGI ON THEIR WAY TO JERUSALEM

new star, very bright and beautiful, was coming. The Magi intended to start on a long journey when it appeared. Where? To Jerusalem, the great city of Hebrew land. Why were they going? Their wise books had told them that a wonderful thing would happen in the Hebrew country while the new star was in the sky. A great King was to be born in Israel, and this beautiful star was the sign that would tell the Magi when the King had come. Would it peep over the hilltops in the early morning, or would it rise out of the East as they watched at midnight? Perhaps just as the sun's last ray had said good night, its first beams

might flash a welcome to the waiting Wise Men.

At last the star appeared, and then the Magi started off on their long journey toward Jerusalem. How far they traveled and how long it took them to reach that distant city no one knows. Weary men they must have been as their tired camels passed through the gates to the city of Jerusalem.

Straight to the palace of wicked King Herod they went. "We have seen in the East a wonderful star," they told Herod, "the star which brings good news of a Child born to be the King of the Jews." Herod was troubled. He did not want to

24

hear of any other king in his country. "Tell us where we can find this King, for we have come to honor Him," the Magi said to Herod.

Wicked King Herod was badly frightened at their message. These strangers from the East had been watching the stars and had learned the story they told. The king did not want to lose his throne. What could he do to keep it? Herod called the lawyers and the chief priests to his palace. "Tell me," he demanded, "where do our writings say Christ is to be born?"

"In Bethlehem of Judea," they answered.

When the people of the king's court heard the news the Magi brought they were worried instead of glad.

Herod was troubled. He called the Magi to him secretly and said, "Tell me when you first saw this star."

Men as wise as the Magi could easily see that the wicked king was afraid. The king could not deceive them. When he told them that he, too, wanted to go and worship the new King of the Jews, they must have known his words were not true.

Herod was afraid of the little Child the Wise Men had come to see. He really believed that this little Child was Christ—the Christ whose kingdom was going to over-throw all other kingdoms and whose rule would have no end. Everything wicked has to die, and Herod knew that he was a very, very wicked man. If the Magi would only tell him where he could find that Child, he would surely destroy him.

The Magi must have felt sad as they turned away from Herod's palace. Through the gates of Jerusalem and down the rocky road they and their camels traveled. They were going toward Bethlehem. No welcome from His own people was waiting for the Christ Child. These men were strangers from the East who welcomed Him. They had journeyed over mountains, crossed deserts, and forded rivers that they might bring to the little new-born King their rich gifts. But their hearts were cheered, for high in the heavens rode the glowing star. Not only in the East, but here, it still was guiding them. With the star before them there could be no room in their hearts for anything but joy.

At last the Wise Men reached the little town of Bethlehem. The brightly shining star hung in the heavens above them as they rode softly through the silent streets. The Magi stopped at a house. It must have been a little one, but I know it was clean and looked as homes always do where there is a great deal of love.

THE MAGI BOWED LOW BEFORE THE CHILD JESUS
AS HE LAY ASLEEP IN HIS MOTHER'S ARMS

WICKED KING HEROD

In they went and found the little Child Jesus, and His mother, Mary. It may be that the real King of the Jews lay asleep in His mother's arms when the Magi entered. They bowed low before Him. As Mary watched, the Magi spread before her the gifts they had brought for the Child — gold, rich spices, and sweet-smelling incense. And now the Wise Men were ready to return to the East.

But these students of the stars believed that God spoke to them in dreams. A dream had warned them that the Child Jesus was in danger from Herod. They believed it was God speaking, so they went back to their own country by another road that did not lead through Jerusalem.

"Go away, go away, you can't play with us!" I heard a shrill voice shout under my window.

"What can the matter be?" I wondered as I looked outside. One sulky-looking little fellow was hanging over the fence watching the boys at play in the yard. "Boys," I asked, "why don't you let Willie in the game? He looks lonely."

"He doesn't play fair. We won't have him," little Dick answered.

Then I went back to the story I was writing, the one about wicked King Herod. King Herod didn't play fair, either. He cheated everyone. No one could trust him. He pretended to be very glad when the Magi told him about the baby born "King of the Jews." And all the time he was plotting to kill the Child as soon as he could find Him.

Herod wanted to be a great king. He hoped that some day he would be as great as Solomon. Herod was dreadfully afraid that some one might want to be king and take his kingdom away from him. Do you wonder that he trembled with fear when the Magi told him that a new King of the Jews had been born? Herod was so afraid some-one would interfere with him that he even put his wife to death and ordered three of his own sons killed. He thought they might be cheating him. But while he was watching people to find out if they were cheating him, all the time he was cheating others.

Herod was ill when the Magi—the Wise Men from the East—visited him. He really was dying, although he did not know it. No one can be well and happy who is as wicked as Herod was, and does the dreadful things he did. The unhappy king must have watched every day expecting to see the Magi again. He may even have hoped that these wise men would be foolish enough

HEROD STRAINED HIS EYES AFTER THE RIDER OF EVERY CAMEL HE SAW IN THE STREETS

to bring the little Christ Child back with them. Herod no doubt strained his eyes after the rider of every camel that he saw in the streets of Jerusalem. "Surely the Magi will come today, surely they will be here today," Herod must have said to himself as he opened his eyes each morning.

But no Magi came. Their camels were skimming across the hot desert sands on their way to their own country in the East. No second visit did these Wise Men pay the wicked Herod. For God was watching over the baby Jesus, and one night, while the Magi slept, He told them in a dream to go back to their own country another way.

UNHAPPY KING HEROD WAITING FOR THE MAGI TO RETURN

The king was so angry everyone who saw him ran away in terror. How dared these Magi treat a king as if they had no respect for him? When they did not come you cannot imagine how angry he was, and what a terrible thing he planned to do.

Herod knew now that he could live only a few months, perhaps only a few weeks, longer. He felt he must do something and do it at once. He suffered terribly, but that did not make him any kinder, nor did it make him feel sorry that he had been so wicked. Instead, he thought if he must die, he would make a number of other people die. Herod must have said to his friends, "Those Magi think they have fooled me." And I am sure he added under his breath, "I will kill that little new-born King of the Jews if I have to kill all the little boys in Bethlehem."

And that was what he tried to do. As Herod lay dying, a number of little children in Bethlehem were put to death by his orders. The savage king had all the little boys who were two years old and younger destroyed. Think of those sad mothers! There may not have been many of them, but a dozen women crying over their little dead babies is enough to make our hearts ache.

Jesus, the Child who was born "King of the Jews," was not among the murdered children. While King Herod lay dying in his palace, Mary and Joseph were hurrying away to Egypt with their precious Child. The sun shown brightly upon the little family of three as they traveled toward safety. Sunbeams kissed the tiny hands of the Child as he lay asleep in Mary's arms. The same sun shot its golden rays into the room of the wicked Herod and touched his cruel face as he lay dead in the palace.

THE ESCAPE

Let us go back a little and see what had happened in the little house in Bethlehem. Near it we shall see some kneeling camels blinking sleepily as they chew their cud. It is a beautiful night, with many bright stars flashing in the sky. Just above the little house hangs one especially brilliant star like a great electric light held high in the heavens.

Suppose we peep inside the house. Everything is so quiet the people who live there must all be asleep. We will tiptoe quietly through the door and look around. But there's no use in looking for chairs to sit on. People in the country where the little house stands never use chairs. There when the people are tired and want to rest they squat on their heels or sit on the floor.

There are some queer-looking lamps on a stand. You and I would say they were only saucers with handles. The lamps are filled with oil and bits of something that looks like cotton are floating in the oil.

The people in the house are wide awake instead of being asleep as we had thought. Suppose we watch to see what they are doing. A mother is holding a dear little baby folded close in her arms. Why, it is Mary, the maiden who talked with Gabriel!

ONE OF THE MAGI STOPS TO WHISPER SOMETHING TO JOSEPH AS HE STEPS OUTSIDE THE DOOR

She is holding her little son, the promised King. Beside her is a kind-looking man, who must be Joseph, her husband. Then perhaps we may see some strange-looking men saying good-by to Joseph. These men surely do not belong either in Bethlehem or in Jerusalem. No, of course not, for they are the Magi from the East who have brought rich gifts to the infant Jesus. One of the Magi stops to whisper something to Joseph as he steps outside the door. What do you suppose he is saying? Probably he is telling Joseph that Herod wishes to visit the Child Jesus. Joseph knows that no good will come of

THE WISE MEN MOUNT THEIR SLEEPY CAMELS AND
RIDE SILENTLY AWAY

such a visit. If Herod comes to Bethlehem, he will come to do the baby harm.

The Wise Men mount their sleepy camels and ride silently away. How the shells around the camels' necks tinkle as they go strutting down the narrow street! Now, their visitors gone, Joseph and Mary will soon be asleep. The whispered message of the Wise Man made Joseph uneasy. I can almost see him tossing and turning on his hard bed. Suddenly he leaped to his feet and awakened Mary. "We must start at once for Egypt! The Child's life is in danger from Herod."

No doubt Mary anxiously asked why he thought so. I can hear Joseph answer, "An angel from God warned me in a dream to flee into Egypt with you and the Child." I think they must have gone that very night.

Just outside of Bethlehem was an inn, called a khan, where many travelers stopped on their way to Egypt. The little town made a good halting place for people and caravans making a long journey. Here their camels, asses, horses, and other animals could be watered and fed, and the travelers themselves could rest. Joseph may have gone to the khan to see about buying a camel for the journey to Egypt, for he was in a great hurry to be off. He wanted to go the quickest way possible, for they must lose no time in leaving Bethlehem if they were to save the Child from King Herod.

In those days the best way to travel quickly was on a dromedary. These swift, one-humped camels were trained for speed. They never carried baggage, only passengers. We might call a dromedary a "limited express." Because that was the swiftest way to go, I think the little family must have traveled on a dromedary when they fled from King Herod.

It was a long journey to Egypt. An ass would have grown tired, and it would have been thirsty much oftener than Joseph could have found water for it. But dromedaries could go for days without water or food. Another splendid thing was that they could run hour after hour without growing tired. No, I am sure Joseph and Mary, with the Child Jesus, did not wait for a caravan or travel on an ass, but started out that night on a dromedary.

On and on they hurried to reach Egypt and safety. Had the soldiers of King Herod come to Bethlehem in the morning they would have seen only a tiny speck moving rapidly

ON AND ON HURRY JOSEPH AND MARY WITH JESUS

across the distant plain. Little would they have suspected that what they saw disappearing in the distance was the Child they had come to destroy.

It was hot in Egypt and very uncomfortable, and Joseph and Mary were anxious to go back home. They did not have long to wait. In a few months news reached them that Herod had died. Now that the cruel king had gone, they thought the child Jesus would be safe.

Another dream came to Joseph in which an angel told him he might return to Israel with Mary and the Child. And Joseph went at once. How happy Mary and Joseph must have felt as they journeyed, thinking

A DROMEDARY AND ITS MASTER

31

that soon they would be at home again, in the little house. But they could not go back to Bethlehem. Why? Because Herod's son, a man as wicked as his father, was now ruler over Judea. Bethlehem, you know, is in Judea.

Another son of Herod was ruling in Galilee. This son was not so wicked as his father and his brother. So to Nazareth, a pretty little town in Galilee, Joseph carried Mary and her little Son. Here Mary and Joseph had lived before they went to Bethlehem, and here I am sure they lived happily. People whose hearts are as full of love as theirs were can never be unhappy no matter where they may live.

BRINGING WATER FROM THE WELL IN THE LITTLE TOWN OF NAZARETH

IN THE TEMPLE

A long procession was winding slowly through mountain paths and across broad, grassy plains. Snarling camels, keen little donkeys, chattering children, gaily dressed women, and solemn-faced men all together were journeying toward Jerusalem. Behind them followed so many animals that I doubt if you could count them all. Cattle with frightened eyes, skipping lambs, and frisky kids were driven into line when they stopped by the wayside for a nibble of grass or a juicy thistle. The people in this procession were Hebrews making their yearly journey to Jerusalem to keep the Passover in the temple. Every family must sacrifice a lamb on the temple altar. Some people wished to give more than a single lamb, so they brought with them cattle and kids.

Imagine how crowded the big city of Jerusalem was when these thousands of strangers visited it! Every house with an extra bed or a spare room was made ready to welcome a guest. But with everyone willing to entertain a visitor, there still was not enough room inside the walls of Jerusalem to care for all those who came. Did the people who could find no place

CHRIST IN THE TEMPLE

to stay turn around and go back home? No indeed, not a bit of it. They unstrapped their tents from the backs of their camels, set them up in the valley outside the city walls, and at once began housekeeping.

Had you looked over the city walls you might have thought a big army was camped around Jerusalem. But all these people looked so peaceful you wouldn't have been frightened a bit. Some one who wrote a book about these times said that often more than two million people journeyed to Jerusalem for the feast of the Passover. That is

A CAMP OUTSIDE THE WALLS OF JERUSALEM

a greater number of people than live in any of our cities except in the very largest, such as New York or Chicago. We shall not try to count all the caravans in the long line or watch them as they finally reach the city gates. Suppose we look only at the one from Nazareth.

Some of the people in the caravan from Nazareth found a home in Jerusalem during the week of the feast of the Passover. Mary and Joseph were among those who found a stopping place in the city. With them was their son, the boy Jesus. He was twelve years old, and this was his first visit to Jerusalem.

A SCENE IN THE STREETS OF JERUSALEM DURING THE FEAST OF THE PASSOVER

When some of you children visit a big town, what do you do first, and where do you want to go? To a picture show, I suppose, or perhaps to a candy shop, or to a druggist's for an ice-cream cone. In Jerusalem there were gay shops and fine bazaars where many curious articles were sold. But only one spot in all the wonderful city did the little twelve-year-old lad wish to visit. His parents had told Him about the great temple which King Herod had built. They had told Him how all the people were looking for a king who would save them from all their suffering. This boy wished to go only to the temple because he knew that it was God's house.

Soon the week of the Passover ended. All the animals the people had brought with them had been sacrificed upon the altar. Friends who met only once a year at these feasts were saying good-by. Then the gates of Jerusalem were opened wide, and caravan after caravan, on the homeward way, moved slowly down the rocky hillside to the plains below.

Caravans had a habit of starting out on a journey late in the afternoon and stopping at the first well or spring they reached. Whether a caravan traveled all day or rested most

of the day, it was a "day's journey" to the people in it. Thus the people sometimes called only two or three hours' travel a "day's journey."

At the little town of Beeroth (el Bireh) is a fine spring of water. Perhaps the caravan that is on its way to Nazareth will camp there, because it is the best stopping place for travelers who are going there. Sure enough, the caravan halts at Beeroth. Mary and Joseph miss their son and go from friend to friend hoping to find Him. He is not with any of the caravans. They think that He must still be in Jerusalem, so back to the city they hurry.

MARY AND JOSEPH HURRYING BACK TO THE CITY TO FIND THEIR SON

35

Three long, anxious days they try to find Jesus. Finally they go back to the temple. And there they find him. He is sitting among the grave men who taught the Law, asking them many questions. He answers questions, too. The wise lawyers are astonished at the wisdom of the boy. His clear, truthful eyes looking into theirs must make them ashamed of some of their acts and thoughts. Herod chose the priests, and he did not always choose honest ones. All those who belonged to Herod's family liked only the people who worked for them. They did not like anyone who worked for God. But this boy is on God's side, every one of the lawyers and priests He met in the temple could tell that.

"Son, why hast thou thus dealt with us?" his mother asks him. "Behold thy father and I sought thee sorrowing."

Mary and Joseph were greatly astonished to find their son in the temple talking so wisely with the teachers.

The lad was surprised that they should have looked for him so long. Where should his parents expect to find him? Surely they should know he would be in the temple. So Jesus said to his mother: "How is it that ye sought me? Did ye not know that I must be about my Father's business?"

But He was only twelve years old, just a boy, and the Law He loved told Him He must obey his parents. And so He left the great temple and went back to Nazareth with them. As they traveled homeward under the friendly stars, Mary wondered in her heart over the words of wisdom the Child had spoken. She may have put her arm around the slight figure of the sweet-faced boy as He walked beside her. He was her son, but from His eyes shone the spirit of the Son of God.

"SON, WHY HAST THOU DEALT THUS WITH US?"
ASKED MARY

LOCUSTS AND WILD HONEY

How many of you little people like to be tumbled out of bed for a morning walk so early that the sun hasn't yet chased all the darkness out of the sky? I'm going to ask those little folks who like tramping in the cool, dewy morning to take a walk, with me. It is just a "pretend" walk, of course, but you and I know very well what good times we can have just pretending.

Put on your boots. No, not those common school shoes! Fairy boots, I mean. We wear fairy boots when we pretend. With our boots on, let us step right across the United States. Then let us lift our feet high and take another step and we're over the big ocean. One more long step and we'll find ourselves right where we want to be, near the shore of the Dead Sea.

It is a lonely place. No people live here. Even animals don't seem to like it. Above is the sky, and everywhere are bare rocks. Grass and bushes and a few trees are here, but those only grow along the courses of the streams emptying into the lake. Everywhere else the

OUT IN THE WILDERNESS JOHN WAS UP EARLY AND
OUT OF HIS TENT

rocks and the waves of the sea will tell it to us:

"There was once a man who lived in this wilderness. He wore queer clothes—only a coarse camel's hair shirt, and a rough hair mantle over his shoulders. Sometimes he must have been very cold, especially at night as he lay asleep in his tent. His long hair fell over his shoulders and often blew in his eyes, very much as Elijah's did. He was always up early and out of his tent before the sun said good morning to the earth.

"Watch! Can't you see him coming down that hill? He thrusts his staff into the holes between the rocks. When that long staff digs deep into the holes there is a whirr of tiny wings and an angry buzzing. The bees think him a meddlesome fellow when he helps himself to the honey they had stored among the rocks. Look at the man's long, lean arm as it carries a dripping bit of honey to his mouth. He must be making his breakfast of it. But what can those queer-looking things be he is eating with the honey? Oh, those are locusts! The people in this part of the country think them a great dainty.

"The man's name is John. An angel gave him that name before he was born. His father Zacharias

ground is scorched and bare, baked as hard as clay marbles by the sun's heat. You can't get cool by drinking from the lake nor by bathing in its clear, beautiful green waters. Some people call it the Salt Sea, for it is saltier than the salt you use on your table. As for bathing! You would bob up and down on the waters like a rubber ball. No drowning in the Salt, or Dead, Sea. The waters hold you up instead of pulling you down. Even though this place is not liked, it has a wonderful story to tell, and we have come here to listen to it. If we listen, the and his mother Elizabeth were very happy because of him. His parents were very old when he was born, and they were surprised when a son was promised them.

"He must have been a strange lad. Why? Because he always liked this wilderness better than big towns or cities. Here in this lonely place he played and grew to be a man. There was too much noise in cities for him. Like Elijah, he preferred to be alone and think about God rather than to live in cities where people quarreled so much of the time. He was getting ready to tell the people that the great and kind King they expected God to send was already among them. John was his herald, sent beforehand to prepare the hearts of the people to receive their King.

"Oh, the country was so wicked and the people in it were so cruel! Poor people had no chance at all. If a person was ill, there was nothing to do but die. No one cared for those who suffered. There were a number of temples and many different gods—the kind of gods people were afraid of and no one loved. Even the Hebrews who had been taught to worship the true God had almost forgotten Him. There did not seem to be any love or sympathy anywhere. If you had traveled the whole length of the land you would have seen nothing but hate and fear, wretched poverty, and dreadful suffering.

"Sometimes John did go into the city. But, like Elijah, he went only to tell the people they were wicked and must do better. He was watching all the time for the coming King. As soon as he had pointed Him out to the people, John's work would be over—but that is another story."

The rocks are silent now, since they have told their story. The waves rippling on the seashore have no more to tell us. Suppose we

THIS SOLDIER HAD NO MERCY FOR THE POOR

JOHN THE BAPTIST RETURNING TO THE WILDERNESS
WHERE HE COULD BE ALONE WITH GOD

step back again to our own country. Church bells are ringing. Happy children are skipping along to Sunday school. Sick little folks are being cared for by sweet-faced nurses in sunny hospitals. Tired animals are being groomed and fed instead of being kicked and beaten. Love seems to be everywhere. And all these changes came about because John the Baptist taught the people to be sorry for and ashamed of their sins. He pointed out to them the One who was their King, and he was not afraid to deliver the message God had sent to the world by him.

KING AND HERALD

One summer morning as the gray dawn, the sun's messenger, was creeping silently over the hot city, I heard the noise of chattering tongues and the patter of feet under my window. Where were the owners of those feet going so early in the morning? And why were they in such a hurry? They were going to the lake, of course, for a dip in its cool waters before the scorching sun came up. All these people, little and big, my ears told me, were happy.

Then I shut my eyes and with my mind saw another lake with a long, winding, yellow river flowing into it. Crowds of people were

IN THE CROWD WERE SCRIBES AND PHARISEES

40

hurrying down to that lake, too, but they did not look happy. This second picture I saw with my eyes closed was not a pretty one. The fierce rays of the sun had burned up nearly everything bordering the bank of the yellow river. Even the ground looked as though it had been baked. Suppose you shut your eyes. Then perhaps you too can see the picture just as I saw it. Bare, bleak-looking hills like stern, grim-faced soldiers stand guard at each side of the yellow river. Keep your eyes closed while we all watch with our minds that long procession of wretched, unhappy people as they come pouring down the steep mountain sides:

There goes a Pharisee wrapping his cloak more closely about him. He is afraid he will touch some one he believes not quite so good as himself. Why is he here? He has come to listen to a great preacher. Can you guess who it is? A sick-looking beggar goes stumbling slowly along and is rudely shoved to one side by a sneering Sadducee. Scribes in silken robes carefully pick their way through the sun-baked plain. A spot on their white gowns seems worse to them than the hearts of stone they carry in their breasts. We see here soldiers with shining spears and glittering helmets,

TO THE LAKE WENT OLD MEN WITH STAFFS AND SOLDIERS WITH SWORDS AND SHINING HELMETS

and greedy tax-gatherers holding their purses with long, lean fingers. Rich men on camels, and old men with staffs in their hands are hurrying toward the river, all of them anxious to get there.

Why are such crowds going to this desolate and lonely place? We can see no houses, nor even tents. Even the trees have given up trying to live in this desolate region. Surely all these people are on the way to see something or some one. Yes, there, standing on the brink of the river, is the man they are coming to see. He looks like the man we saw eating his breakfast of locusts and honey! I am sure it is John the Baptist.

Everyone seems interested. What can he be saying? He is talking to them about trees, and telling them that an unfruitful tree is useless and ought to be cut down and burned. The Baptist says that all wicked people, like unfruitful trees, are good for nothing. Scribe and Pharisee scowl. Are they asking one another if John means them, because they do so little good to others?

He urges the people to be baptized to show that they are sorry for their sins. "Wash all the bad and wicked wishes out of your hearts. Show by being baptized that you intend to stop sinning," is John's word to the people. "Stop wanting to cheat people when you collect taxes, and take from them only what they owe," John tells the tax collector. To the soldier he says, "Be kinder, tell the truth about others, and don't grumble about your wages." But John doesn't pay much attention to the proud Pharisee and scoffing Sadducee. He calls them children of vipers. Why? They pretend to be, oh, so very, very good, and many of them are not half so good as some of the poor people they have shut up in prison.

John seems to be waiting for some one. So do the people. All of them are looking for the promised King. While they wait there by the riverside the King comes. He doesn't look a bit like one, and so no one but John knows Him. The people see only a stranger from Nazareth, whose father, Joseph, is a carpenter. This strange man a king! Why, kings have rich purple robes and wear golden crowns! To the people this kindly Galilean, whose eyes seem to see the very thoughts in one's mind, looks just like one of themselves. The Stranger is not even rich, for instead of riding he walks.

Jesus, the Nazarene, has come to be baptized by John. The people no doubt are thinking that no King would come to see John. By what sign shall they know that this simple Galilean is really the expected King? John, the herald of the King, will tell them. And he does. "Behold the Lamb of God!" John says, pointing to Jesus as He walks by the riverside.

John's great message has been given. He has opened the way for the King. The "Lamb of God" was the great King who came to love all the people in the world, and, by loving them, to save them from their sins.

JESUS HAS COME DOWN TO THE JORDAN TO BE BAPTIZED BY JOHN

A CHRISTMAS CAROL

The Christ-child lay on Mary's lap,
　His hair was like a light.
(O weary, weary were the world,
　But here is all aright.)

The Christ-child lay on Mary's breast,
　His hair was like a star.
(O stern and cunning are the kings,
　But here the true hearts are.)

The Christ-child lay on Mary's heart,
　His hair was like a fire.
(O weary, weary is the world,
　But here the world's desire.)

The Christ-child stood at Mary's knee,
　His hair was like a crown,
And all the flowers looked up at Him,
　And all the stars looked down.

—GILBERT K. CHESTERTON

A CHRISTMAS FOLK-SONG

The Little Jesus came to town;
The wind blew up, the wind blew down;
Out in the street the wind was bold;
Now who would house Him from the cold?

Then opened wide a stable door,
Fair were the rushes on the floor;
The Ox put forth a hornèd head:
"Come, little Lord, here make Thy bed."

Uprose the sheep were folded near:
"Thou Lamb of God, come, enter here."
He entered there to rush and reed,
Who was the Lamb of God indeed.

The Little Jesus came to town;
With ox and sheep He laid Him down;
Peace to the byre, peace to the fold,
For that they housed Him from the cold!

—LIZETTE WOODWORTH REESE

A CHILD'S GIFT

All bring the Christ child presents:
　The poorest does his part;
And I, who am so little,
　Give to Him my heart.

—KATHARINE LEE BATES

GLAD TIDINGS OF
GREAT JOY

While shepherds watched their flocks
　　by night,
　All seated on the ground,
The angel of the Lord came down,
　And glory shone around.

"Fear not," said he, for mighty dread
　Had seized their troubled mind;
"Glad tidings of great joy I bring
　To you and all mankind.

"To you, in David's town, this day
　Is born of David's line
A Saviour who is Christ the Lord;
　And this shall be the sign:

"The heavenly babe you there shall find
　To human view display'd,
All meanly wrapped in swathing bands,
　And in a manger laid."

Thus spake the seraph; and forthwith
　Appear'd a shining throng
Of angels praising God, who thus
　Address'd their joyful song:

"All Glory be to God on high,
　And to the earth be peace;
Good will henceforth from Heav'n
　　to men
　Begin and never cease."

—NATHAN TATE

44

THE EARLY WORK OF JESUS

"DRAW NOW," JESUS COMMANDS THE SERVANTS, "AND BEAR UNTO THE RULER OF THE FEAST."

WINE AND WATER

How would you all like to go to a wedding? Would you not like to be in the procession? Can you carry a lamp? There is no use in your trying to join this wedding procession unless you carry one. No! No! Don't try to carry the tall piano lamp, nor reach for the big one that stands on the table. Go up into your great-grandmother's attic and perhaps you will find hidden away in her chests something in which you can carry a light. Yes, that deep old bronze saucer with a handle will do nicely. Fill it with oil and let a wick float in it. Now you are ready.

The procession will be noisy. There will be music, singing, and shouting. The more noise you can make the better. If you make a great deal of noise, the bridegroom will feel sure you are enjoying his wedding.

Now the procession is ready to start. First come the band and the singers. Then follow the torchbearers. The last to appear are the bridegroom and his friends. All of them will go to the bride's house. She will be waiting for this merry company, she and her bridesmaids.

The bridegroom is coming to take her to his own home, where he will give a splendid feast to all the company. If you should be allowed to peep inside the bride's room you would think you were looking at a snowbank. You might walk all around this bank of white to find the bride's face. But it would be of no use. No one, not even the bridegroom, can get a glimpse of her face until after the marriage feast. Her great white veil covers her all over from top to toe.

Weddings in this strange country of Palestine are at night. That is why the guests in the procession must carry lights. No fear of our missing the bridegroom's house as we come back with the bride! Lighted lanterns will be strung across the street and swing back and forth before his house.

No one will ever forget the wedding to which I have asked you to go. A Guest has been invited who loves to help all people. No matter what their trouble may be, He will always help them out of it. He sits among the merry throng with His mother and His disciples. I do not doubt that He laughs and talks with all of them. Since in His heart there is always a wish to help, I am sure everyone who comes near Him is helped and feels better because He is there. We know who that kindly Guest is. It is Jesus. Beside Him is Mary, His mother.

In the midst of the merrymaking

something dreadful happens. In Palestine people think it a misfortune for the wine to give out before the guests have had their feast. Mary is watching the steward of the feast. "They have no more wine," she whispers to Jesus. But why does she tell Him? The bridegroom is the one to supply the wine. How can Jesus, who is only a guest, help them out of their trouble? We shall see. Standing near Him are some empty jars. "Fill them with water," He says to the servants. And they obey. "Draw now," He commands, "and bear unto the ruler of the feast."

The steward, who is the "ruler of the feast," must be very much pleased as he tastes the delicious wine. Six jars of this rich wine now are waiting for the guests. Only a moment before the jars held sparkling water. Now they are brimming with wine. The steward praises the bridegroom for keeping his best wine until the end of the feast. Neither he nor the bridegroom knows how the wine came there. But the servants who put water into the jars and drew out wine know, and I am sure they will tell all their friends about it. The Guest from Galilee has done this wonder. No one there suspects that He is King. Why? Because one who helps others is not the people's idea of a king.

BETHESDA—HOUSE OF MERCY

If I should say "swimming pool," how many of you little folks, especially you boys, would prick up your ears and listen? Eyes of black, blue, and gray would dance and sparkle, for the owners of those eyes know how delicious is a plunge in the cool water. But how would you like to lie near a great pool of water and never be able to get into it? No fun in that, is there?

Put on those fairy boots again, the ones we used when we stepped across America and the ocean into a strange country. Now come with me to a large pool of water in that same country. Around the pool there are five big porches with marble pillars. Lying about the pillars are some wretched people. They are poor and ill. See that feeble old man groping for a pillar against which he may lean. He must be blind! A ragged, crippled boy is hobbling along on crutches. What can they want here? Do you suppose they come here because it is cooler, just as we go to the parks on a hot summer day? Perhaps that is one of the reasons. But there is another reason. Sometimes the water in the pool is shallow and at other times it is deep. Whenever the water changes and becomes deep all these people rush into it. Why? Because this pool of Bethesda, after the water has changed, is supposed to cure the first person who steps into it. But think of that poor blind man and crippled boy! How can they find the way in? No one in this country cares about them. Who will help the feeble ones who have no friends?

Across the porch and between the pillars comes One whose eyes are always looking for those people whom everyone else forgets. His ears will hear the weakest voice calling for help. Who can He be? "Jesus of Nazareth passeth by," the people will tell you. And as He

JESUS AND THE MAN WHO WAS HEALED AT THE POOL OF BETHESDA

goes by He leaves health and joy. Of course Jesus will stop beside the most miserable of all these poor people gathered about the pool. One poor fellow has been ill so long that during his illness you would have had time to grow from a baby into a man. Just think of it!

"Do you wish to be well?" Jesus asks him.

"Yes," answers the man, "but I cannot get into the pool quickly and somebody always gets in ahead of me."

How pitiful! That poor man, with his shrunken arms and twisted feet, and his weak body, is too feeble to do anything but lie quietly near the pool. Every time the water

"DO YOU WISH TO BE WELL? JESUS ASKED THE MAN

changed he hoped that someone would be kind and help him into the pool. How glad he must be to hear the voice of Jesus saying to him, "Arise, take up thy bed, and walk." Imagine his astonishment as his weak back straightens and grows strong. The twisted feet are whole and step firmly upon the ground. He stands up a well man and gathers his bed in his arms. That is not so hard a task as you might think, for his bed is only a rug of wool or sheepskin.

Passing back and forth among the porches are priests, Pharisees, and publicans. Doctors of the law and busy merchants also are there. Bethesda is a place where people gather, much as they do in our parks. Rich and poor, young and old, tired mothers, and happy girls and boys pass the pool. Yet among them all there is only One who came to help.

Suppose when we step back to our own country we bring back with us some of the water of Bethesda! No, not the real water, of course! But a little spot in our hearts warm with love for people and the wish to help them. Bethesda, you know, means "House of Mercy." And it was by this pool of "mercy" that the sick man heard the voice of Jesus.

THROUGH THE ROOF

Who lives in the house next door to you? Is it a big house or a little house? I hope it is a big one with little children in it. When I was a small girl, I can remember thinking that people who lived in houses without children were stupid. If your little friends next door ask you to visit them, you probably take your best doll or a bag of marbles, walk up the steps, knock on the door, and go in. But suppose, when you went visiting, there was such a crowd around the door that you could not get into the house. What would you do? There! I'll have to put my hands over my ears, for you'll all be shouting at once, "Go home, of course, and come some other day."

In our country that would be the proper thing to do. But in Palestine, where Jesus lived, people sometimes did strange things when they wanted to see Him. If they could find no other way, they even came into a house through the roof!

Watch that little house in the narrow city street. You may think there is a wedding or a party going on in it. People are packed so close together by the doorway that no late comer can enter. Even the windows are filled with people, looking out

CARRYING A MAN SICK OF THE PALSY TO JESUS
TO ASK FOR HELP

Along the street come four men. They walk slowly and carefully. They are carrying a bed on which lies a man who has palsy. That is, he can move only with the help of other people. He can do nothing for himself. The men reach the door. Will the crowd stand aside and let the four men pass with their helpless friend? No, they are so anxious to get help for themselves that I don't believe they even see the helpless man on the bed. Doorway and windows are packed with people. Not one more can enter, and here are five men who need to get to Jesus to ask for help.

at the crowds pushing and struggling to get inside the house.

Jesus is in that little house. People for miles around have heard that He is there and have come to see Him. Through the street they hurry toward the house. If you should turn and look round and round you would see people coming from every direction. Scribes, Pharisees, and rulers are there. As usual they are finding fault because Jesus helps wicked people as well as good ones. The poor, the rich, and the ill, all have come to ask Jesus for something. And not one among them offers Him anything in return.

DOWN THROUGH THE ROOF THE MEN LOWER THE
HELPLESS MAN

Will they turn back and come some other day? Surely not. Fortunately this house is only one story high. There are steps leading up to the flat roof. The four men carry the bed up the steps and begin to tear up the roof. Don't frown and say that is not the right way to treat a neighbor's house. Those little houses in Palestine are not built as ours are, and often the roofs can easily be torn apart and as easily put together again.

The house we are watching must have such a roof, for not one of the crowd, not even the owner, seems to notice that a hole is being made in it. When the roof is opened, down, down the four men lower the helpless man. Right at the feet of Jesus

THROWING HIS BED OVER HIS SHOULDER THE ONCE HELPLESS MAN WALKED OUT OF THE DOOR

he rests. Can't you see those four friends on the roof peering through the hole they have made, anxiously watching what is happening in the room below?

Isn't that a strange way of seeking help—just to open the roof and place the helpless man directly in front of Jesus? The four men are so sure that Jesus will cure the man the instant He sees him, that they do not even think it necessary to speak. Jesus is pleased with their faith in Him. We all like to be trusted, and all of us are hurt, just as Jesus must have been, by unkind words such as the Scribes and Pharisees were always speaking about Him.

Jesus rewards the faith of the helpless man and his friends, for He says to him, "Take up your bed and walk."

Up springs the once helpless man. He throws his bed, which is only blankets, over his shoulder and walks briskly toward the door. No need of going up through the roof to get out. The crowd is so astonished to see the once helpless man walking, that it melts away from the doorway and allows the man to pass out and join his four friends who are waiting outside for him. As the men walk away you can hear the crowd saying, "We never saw anything like this before."

HER ONLY SON

Tap, tap, tap! "What is that? Some one must be knocking at my door," you say. Yes, it is I, come to take you for another walk through the country of Palestine. What shall we see today? Another procession. No, not a wedding this time. The people in this procession are all walking slowly. Some are crying. Through the narrow and often dirty streets of the little town of Nain they move toward the city gate.

See that poor woman dressed all in black. Her hair looks as if she had forgotten to comb it. She must have put ashes on her head. In Palestine when people are so un-happy that no one can comfort them, they cover their heads with ashes.

Sometimes they tear their clothes and lie with their faces on the ground. We know something sad has happened to this woman. How her feet drag as she walks along! And her shoulders are bent as though under a heavy load. A kind-hearted neighbor has an arm around her and is trying to help her.

If you and I look carefully at this procession, we shall find out where it is going and why the people are so sad. In our own country you have seen sick people carried to the hospitals on stretchers. Something that looks like a stretcher is being carried by some men in the procession. There is a young man lying on it, but he is not ill. He died last night, and his friends are carrying him out of the

THIS UNHAPPY MOTHER, A WIDOW OF NAIN, HAS
LOST HER ONLY SON

but the sound of their voices tells us they are happy. In the midst of the crowd is a noble figure in white. The multitudes that follow crowd about Him and His disciples. The sun touches His hair as if in blessing, and sheds a glorious light on all who follow Him. The sad procession of black-robed mourners meets the company of people who are light-hearted and cheery. These happy people may not even see the sad mother, or if they do see her they probably are saying, "Why should we stop? We have no friends in this funeral train, and the young man is not a relative of ours."

But One among this lively group will not move on. He stops in the path of the sad procession. The

city to the rocks in the valley. In caves among these rocks are placed the bodies of people who die in Palestine.

The sad procession reaches the city gate and passes on toward the valley. The poor woman is wringing her hands in grief. The lad whose body lies on the bier or stretcher was her only son, and she is a widow. Perhaps there is no one left who will be kind to her and see that she does not starve. She may lose the little one-room house in which she and her son have lived. She has no money to pay the taxes or the rent. She may have to beg the rest of her life.

Coming up the path toward the city we see a very different crowd of people. All of them are excited,

THE MOTHER REJOICING THAT HER SON IS ALIVE

54

stretcher-bearers and the mother, looking up, see Jesus standing there. Some people in the procession have heard that He heals people who are ill. The young man's mother may be thinking. "Oh, if He had only been here before my boy died!"

Jesus touches the stretcher as the procession halts. The young man is dead, the people say. I have no doubt that even the disciples of Jesus wonder why He stops a funeral on its way to a tomb in the valley. Jesus is sorry for the mother. When He is sorry for people He always does something to help them. His words make people who hear them live and become well. "Weep not," He says to the sad mother. Then laying upon the bier His hand, which always brings a blessing when it touches anyone, He says to the young man, "I say unto thee, arise."

The closed eyes open. Into the pale cheeks color comes. The boy sits up and speaks. I should like to have heard the first words he spoke when Jesus gave him back to his mother. They were happy words, I'm sure. Do you suppose that as he looked into the face of Jesus, he recognized the face of the King?

The little procession, now a glad one, turns back into the city. Everyone is happy and is saying in his heart, "God is surely with us."

TOUCHING THE HEM

Come with me to the seashore, little people. No; don't take your buckets and shovels for a play on the sand. You will have no use for them. The seaside you and I will visit is in Palestine, and already there is so large a crowd on the beach that it is a wonder some of the people are not pushed into the water. Among the number on the beach are many people who are ill. All of them, weak and strong, are waiting to welcome some one coming toward them in a boat. One little fellow is holding tight to his mother's hand as they both stand with their feet in the water.

"Mother, do you think Jesus will make my crooked back straight?" he asks her.

"Yes, dear," his mother replies. "Jesus helps all who need Him, and He will see that you need Him."

So that is why such great numbers of people are waiting for the approaching boat. Jesus and some of His disciples are in it. All in this multitude have come to meet Jesus. Many of them have come to ask Him to cure either themselves or some friend or relative they have brought with them. Each person is anxious to reach the water's edge and be the first one to speak to

PETER SHOVED THE BOAT AWAY FROM THE PEOPLE
ON THE SHORE

loves all of them and enjoys giving good things to them.

See that proud Pharisee scornfully drawing around him his rich robe with its wide hem and silken fringe! He is afraid that some one whom he thinks not quite so good as himself, might touch him. How the people push and crowd one another! I hope the mothers have left their babies at home, for they surely would be crushed in the frantic efforts all are making to reach the boat.

Suddenly the crowd separates and a path is made straight through it toward the boat. Somebody very important must be coming. Yes, it is a rich ruler who wishes to speak with Jesus, and everyone in his path steps hastily aside to let him pass.

"Come with me," the ruler begs Jesus. "My little daughter is dying and only you can help her."

Off Jesus and His disciples start to the ruler's house. Many in the multitude follow them.

Watch! Following the people is a woman. How pale and weak she is! She is ill, and often leans upon the arm of a friend who is with her. She isn't as important as the ruler, and the people do not step aside to let her pass toward Jesus. But she needs His help as

Jesus. And each in his haste and eagerness to be first joggles his neighbors and shoves his elbows into their sides.

The boat touches the shore. There is a mighty rush of anxious people toward it. How can the Master hear when all of them speak at once? And how can He stand so quietly when they rudely push against Him? Look! Peter is shoving the boat away from the shore, so that Jesus and His disciples can sit in it comfortably, away from the anxious rabble. Jesus heals all who come to Him. He never seems to grow tired. I think it must be because He really much as the great ruler's little daughter.

Will she be strong enough to push her way through that crowd? Her friend thinks not, and urges her to go home and wait until some other day. "Tomorrow there may not be so big a crowd," her friend says.

"I must reach Him today, I *shall* reach Him today," the woman replies. "For twelve long years I have been ill," she adds. "I have spent all my money trying to get well, and have only grown worse."

"If you have been ill for so long you surely can wait a few days more before asking Jesus to help you," said the friend again urging her to go home.

"No, no, it must be today, it *will* be today," replies the woman earnestly.

On she presses and leaves her doubting companion behind. "I shall reach Him, I shall reach Him," she is thinking as she moves unsteadily through the mass of hurrying people. She is close, so close to the Master that her feeble fingers rest for an instant on the hem of His flowing robe. "If I may only touch the border of His robe I shall be cured," she has been thinking. She has touched the hem and turns to go away, for through her body

"IF I MAY ONLY TOUCH THE BORDER OF HIS ROBE
I SHALL BE CURED," THOUGHT THE WOMAN

she feels the strength and glow of health.

Only a slight touch by a feeble hand on the hem of His garment, but it causes Jesus to pause and ask who touched Him. He turns around and sees the happy woman. He speaks to her, and she tells Him of her many years of suffering, and how she has been healed just by touching the hem of His garment. Few people have such trust in Him, and I can see a shade of sadness in the eyes of Jesus as He looks kindly upon the woman. His sweet, clear voice is saying to her, "Daughter, go in peace, your faith has made you well."

SUPPER TIME

Let us go to a wonderful picnic. The biggest picnic you ever attended was not half so large as the one we shall pretend to visit this afternoon. When you and I go to picnics we carry baskets filled with good things to eat. We look for a tree under whose spreading branches we may eat our lunch. My, how good everything tastes! Mother knew we would be hungry when she filled those baskets.

At the wonderful picnic we are pretending to visit we should have found nothing to eat. Plenty of baskets were there—large ones—some made of ropes twisted together, all smelling of fish, and every one empty. Imagine going to a picnic with empty baskets! "What a queer picnic!" some little folks are thinking. What a strange picnic! Never before had there been one like it, and never since has there been another like it. The picnic was on a lonely hillside near a lake in Palestine, that sad country where poor people had no friends and many sick people had no one to help them. Only Jesus felt sorry for them, and always gave the people exactly what they needed.

That is why on the day of the picnic Jesus and His disciples were crowded almost into the water by the eager people who pushed and shoved one another as they tried to reach Jesus where He stood on the shore.

"We have had no time to eat or rest," said the disciples at last.

"We will go into a quiet place and rest," Jesus answered.

Into a boat they climbed, and rowed across the lake. But the people wouldn't be left behind. They could walk around the lake to the lonely hillside, and that is what they did. When Jesus and His disciples came to the spot, they found a multitude of people waiting for them there.

How disappointed the tired disciples must have been! I don't believe they gave the hungry multitude a hearty welcome. Perhaps it made some of them cross to hear the people asking for help when they themselves were so tired. But Jesus smiled. He must have held out his hand in friendly welcome. I can see a mother bringing her blind baby to Him for healing. There is a cripple dragging himself along the ground, asking that he might be made to walk. Some of the people were carried on stretchers. They held out their shriveled arms toward Jesus, the only friend who had ever shown pity for them. He healed them all.

JESUS FEEDING FIVE THOUSAND PEOPLE

A MOTHER BRINGING HER BLIND BABY TO JESUS
FOR HEALING

The sun turned scarlet and long shadows began to creep over the grassy hillside. Why didn't all those hungry people hurry home and buy something to eat before the shops in town were closed?

We know that was what the disciples thought, for they asked Jesus to send the people away, as night was near.

"The people are tired, and many of them have come a long way. I cannot send them away hungry. Give ye them to eat," said Jesus.

"How can we feed all these hungry people when we have nothing to give them?" asked the disciples. And they added, "If we went to town and bought food for them it would cost too much." It would have cost them two hundred shillings, and that means about thirty-four dollars of our money.

The sun was slipping out of sight, and soon darkness would begin to settle over the valley. Sleepy babies probably were crying, and other little folks were teasing their mothers to hurry home so they could eat their bowls of porridge.

But Jesus would not send the people home. He intended to feed them and to fill their empty baskets. "How much food is there here?" asked Jesus of the disciples. "Go and see."

"Five loaves and two fish are all we can find," replied the disciples.

"Bring them to me, and ask the people to sit down," commanded Jesus.

The disciples obeyed, probably wondering how Jesus was going to feed five thousand people with five round cakes of bread and two small fish.

Jesus took the bread and fish and blessed them and gave thanks. The watching people and the disciples too, perhaps, were thinking, "How could one be thankful with so little to eat and so many to feed?" As they watched Jesus break the bread and fish into pieces, their eyes must have opened wider and wider, for the more He broke them the bigger grew the piles of food.

The disciples were busy giving the people all they could eat. Perhaps for some it was the first time they had ever had enough for supper. In Jesus' hands the loaves and fishes kept increasing as he broke them into pieces. And those empty baskets the people had brought with them came in handy, for twelve baskets full of bread and fish were left after the people had had enough.

Then down the steep, lonely hillside the people walked, busily talking together as they went. Perhaps a woman is telling her neighbor that she believes Jesus is the promised King. Others are whispering among themselves. "This is of a truth the Prophet that cometh into the world."

THE PEOPLE WENT HOME CARRYING BASKETS FILLED WITH BREAD AND FISH

AFRAID

How the wind did blow! It sent the fisher boy's cap spinning along the beach and nearly tore off the Pharisee's long robe. The sea tossed up and down, for all the waves, little and big, were having a great frolic with the wind. Even the moon smiling down upon the lively waves did not make the sea seem any calmer.

You and I would have preferred to stay on land on such a night. But rough as the sea was, some men seemed anxious to venture out upon it. They were Jesus' disciples. He had told them to cross to the other side of the lake, and thus get away from the crowd. Late that afternoon, with only five loaves and two small fish they, at Jesus' command had fed five thousand people. Now all had had enough to eat and it was growing dark, yet the people did not want to go home. Since they could not stay there all night, Jesus had said to His disciples, "Get into your boat and row across the lake. I will send the people away."

I have often wondered how Jesus managed to get that great throng of people to leave Him and go to their homes. But they finally did go home. Perhaps it was chilly along the shore and the wind blew too strong for them. Or they may have remembered that at home there were other people who were ill whom to-morrow they could bring to Jesus to be healed.

At last Jesus was alone. He turned from the shore and walked

JESUS PRAYING ON THE LONELY HILLSIDE

toward a lonely hillside. No one would care to follow Him into the mountains on such a disagreeable night. How cold and dreary it must have been! But it was the only place where Jesus could pray without being disturbed.

The moon hurried along its nightly path across the sky as if it were anxious to get away from the angry wind. At last it dropped down behind the hills. The morning stars had begun to twinkle when Jesus ceased praying and looked toward the lake. There, tossed about in their little boat, were His disciples. Although they rowed with all their strength, their boat did not seem to move far through those rocking waters. The wind blew them back, and it was not easy for the disciples to pull against it.

Wild winds and waves did not hinder Jesus. He saw that His disciples needed Him and off He started to help them. There was no boat for Him. His disciples had taken the only one. Out on the stormy sea Jesus stepped and walked toward the tossing boat.

The disciples must have been watching the shore, for they saw Him coming. At first they did not know Him, and they were badly frightened. Never before had they seen anyone walking on the sea. I suppose some

OUT ON THE STORMY SEA JESUS STEPPED

of them dropped their oars from fright and crouched down in the bottom of the boat. Their fear soon left them, for they heard a well-known voice calling out to them, "It is I; be not afraid."

While every one of the disciples knew that voice belonged to Jesus, Peter was the first to answer. But Peter usually did speak first. He said to Jesus, "If it is you, tell me to walk on the water to meet you."

And Jesus answered, "Come."

Out of the boat Peter scrambled and stepped bravely upon the sea. He walked forward easily, so easily, indeed, that he had time to notice how strong the wind was and how madly the waters raged. But the moment he noticed the wildness of the storm he was afraid, and then of course he began to sink. He called to Jesus to save him, and Jesus stretched out His hand and caught him.

Do you think Jesus said, "Peter, it was foolish for you to try to walk on the water. You should have known that you could not do it"? No, indeed! Jesus never discouraged people in that way. Instead, Jesus must have looked sad when He said to Peter, "You have little faith. Why were you afraid?"

Then both of them stepped into the boat. The wind died down and the stormy waves grew quiet. The golden rays of the rising sun flashed across the lake as at last the little boat came safely to land, and Jesus and His disciples were at home.

THE LITTLE BOAT CAME SAFELY TO LAND

MY NEIGHBOR

How many of you little people have neighbors? All of you, of course. "The little girl across the street and the boy next door are our neighbors," you say. Palestine, the country where Jesus lived, and where you and I have been visiting so often, had many people in it, and of course many of these people were neighbors.

But would you believe it? There lived a lawyer in Palestine who did not know who his neighbors were, and he asked Jesus to tell him.

Suppose we journey today down the steep, rocky road that leads from Jerusalem to Jericho. We shall all go together. It is safer than traveling alone, for the road is rough and dangerous. Many wild beasts prowl about, and robbers hide in the caves by the roadside and pounce upon lonely travelers. It is best to leave all our valuables behind us. We shall carry nothing that will tempt a thief.

Now we are ready and off we start. Soon the road turns into a solitary place where we can see nothing but high rock walls around us and the blue sky overhead.

This must be the place. Yes, I am sure this is the very spot where a Hebrew traveling all alone from Jerusalem to Jericho was attacked by thieves. His clothes were torn off him and his money was stolen. The cruel thieves beat the poor man and left him lying by the roadside. Suppose we sit here in this cool cave and eat our lunch while I tell you what happened next.

The wounded Hebrew lay groaning where he had been left to die. Surely some one would hear his groans and come to help him. At last a priest came slowly along. He was on the opposite side of the road from the man. The priest heard the moans and looked toward the helpless man. Did he cross over to the side of the injured traveler? No! The priest looked at the man carefully, then drew his robe more closely around him and passed by on the way to Jericho. Why was he so cruel? He did not think he was cruel. He only thought as he went onward, "That man is not one of my neighbors. He is a stranger to me. Why should I stop to help him?"

Late in the afternoon a Levite, or teacher, came hurrying along the road. He was anxious to get out of that desolate valley before nighttime. He paused when he reached the wounded Hebrew. The Levite was interested. He crossed over to the side of the man, who was now nearly dead. He looked closely at him, then shook his head and turned away without offering any help. The man lying in the road was not another teacher, neither was he one of the Levite's neighbors. "It is growing late and I must hurry to a place of safety and shelter," I know the teacher was thinking.

And he probably added as he disappeared down the road, "I should be foolish to stay in this dangerous spot just to help a stranger."

Nightfall was near. Cold winds began to blow through the valley. How the injured man must have shivered! He heard the howl of a wolf in the distance. The savage beast was waiting for darkness, when he would creep up and tear the man in pieces.

Then the last rays of the setting sun shone upon a donkey and his rider. The little animal was trotting merrily along, and I am sure the Samaritan on his back was whistling.

The Samaritan saw the wounded man. He reined in his donkey, jumped off, and ran to the man's side. The Samaritan saw that the man lying at his feet was a Hebrew. The Samaritans and Hebrews hated each other, and never called each other neighbor. But this Samaritan had so much love in his heart he forgot that the man lying there was a Hebrew.

"This wounded man needs help and I can give it to him," thought the Samaritan. So he helped the Hebrew on the donkey, and walked beside him until they reached an inn. All night he stayed with the man and cared for him. In the morning he left some money with the

THE SAMARITAN GAVE THE LANDLORD SOME MONEY
AND ASKED HIM TO CARE FOR THE HEBREW

LOST AND FOUND

Poor little dog! I knew he was lost the moment I heard him whining at my heels. I spoke coaxingly to the small stray, saying, "Come doggie, doggie! Come home with me and you shall have something to eat." But he would not follow. He only sat still, cocking his head on one side as he looked at me. Some people do not know dog language, but I do. So I understood that, as he thumped his tail on the walk, he was saying, "'Doggie' isn't my name. I can't go with you."

Along came a boy whistling. He called to the dog, "Here, Fido, Fido!" Still the dog did not stir. A little girl came sorrowfully down the road. Then her eyes fell upon the dog and she called, "Frisk, Frisk!" At once the small dog bounded into her arms with delight. So "Frisk" was the dog's name, and he did not intend to follow anyone home until he heard it.

The little girl and her dog made me think of a Bible story. There are other animals besides dogs that know their names and will follow only when they hear them called. In Palestine there are many, many sheep. The shepherds who care for them know all the sheep in their flocks and call each one by its name.

landlord and asked him to take care of the Hebrew until he was able to go home.

Now that the story is finished, we will start back again over the road which runs from Jericho to Jerusalem. The rocks no longer look lonely, and the stones seem to smile. How can they help it, since the glowing sunlight of love for one's neighbor has touched them all?

"Who is my neighbor?" the lawyer asked, and Jesus answered by telling him the story I have told you.

"Why, our neighbor is some one we can help, some one who needs us," every child's voice is answering.

Yes, you are right. And the lawyer thought the same thing as he turned away from Jesus.

Let us visit a sheepfold on a sunny hillside in Palestine. There is only one narrow door in the rough stone wall of the fold. What shall we do if the door is shut? Some small boy will answer, "Climb over the top." Impossible! The tops of the walls are covered with tree branches, prickly brambles, and sharp thorns. Even a wolf coming to steal a lamb doesn't dare jump over. Only a half-starved lion or leopard will leap over the wall and risk getting torn on those thorns.

There! The door of the sheepfold opens and out comes the shepherd. His rough sheepskin mantle is thrown over his shoulders. As the day is hot, he wears the fleece outside. Tonight, if he sleeps on the hillside,

NOW AND THEN THE SHEPHERD STOPS AND CALLS SOFTLY TO A STRAYING LAMB

he will turn his mantle inside out and wear the woolly side next to him. He carries a sling, a queer-looking wallet filled with coarse food, and a long crook or staff.

One by one the sheep come through the gate and follow the shepherd. He knows where there is a fine pasture filled with tempting grass. A sparkling stream of cool water gurgles its way across the green field. It is a long way to that pasture. The sheep will have to travel through a lonesome, rocky valley before they reach it. But the shepherd goes before them. Now and then he calls a straying lamb, and the lamb hears and trots obediently after him.

ONE BY ONE THE SHEEP FOLLOW THE SHEPHERD THROUGH THE GATE

67

The shepherd must have sharp eyes. Beside that pool of water among the rocks a savage leopard may be hiding, or a wolf may be watching to see at what moment it can run off with some foolish lamb that lingers behind the flock. The shepherd must watch for these wild beasts and drive them away.

But the pasture is reached at last. And my! oh, my! what a frolic the lambs are having! They kick up their heels and skip about as though they were happy children.

At last the shepherd looks at the sky and calls to his sheep. They are a long way from home and the fold. It is late afternoon, and a storm is coming. Off they move homeward.

THE SHEPHERD SEIZED THE LOST SHEEP, THREW IT ACROSS HIS SHOULDERS AND STARTED FOR THE FOLD

Again they pass safely through the rocky valley.

The gatekeeper opens the door of the sheepfold when he sees them coming. The shepherd stands by the open door with his rod raised. One by one, the sheep and lambs pass under the rod and through the gate into the fold. Hear the shepherd counting the sheep as they pass in, "Ninety-seven, ninety-eight, ninety-nine—"; then he drops his rod and exclaims, "Only ninety-nine sheep! One must be lost. I had a hundred with me this morning."

Do you suppose he says, "One sheep doesn't count for much. I have ninety-nine in the fold, and that is enough"? Indeed not! At once he does what we all do when we lose something. We go out and hunt for it until we find it.

Off the shepherd goes in the darkness and storm, calling the missing sheep by name as he feels his way along the rough valley. He stops. A faint "ba-a-a" reaches his ear. The lost sheep must have taken shelter in some cave among the rocks. The shepherd follows the sound of its voice. Yes, there it is, looking out from between the rocks, and crying "ba-a-a" every time it hears its name called. The shepherd seizes it, throws it across his shoulders, and starts for the sheepfold.

He cannot afford to lose one of his sheep. To the shepherd each sheep and each little lamb is valuable and important.

As soon as the shepherd reaches the fold in safety he calls his friends together, crying, "I have found my sheep! I have found my sheep!" And his friends are glad and rejoice with him.

Jesus liked to watch the sheep. He knew that a good shepherd loves each one of his flock. So one day when the Scribes and Pharisees complained because the Master talked and ate with sinners, Jesus said, "The shepherd hunts the lost sheep, not those that are safe in the fold. Sinners and people who are ill are like lost sheep. They are the ones who need to be helped, and they are the ones I came to help."

The proud Pharisee and the scornful Scribe did not spend any time helping others. "We are better than other people," they said, and they even told God so in their prayers. How angry they must have been when Jesus told them that God is like a good shepherd hunting for his lost sheep, and that God rejoices more over ill people made well and wicked people made good than over all the people who think themselves perfect and strong.

THE GRATEFUL STRANGER

Poor, wretched man, standing alone on the shore and watching a great ship sail out to sea! On that ship are his wife, his children, and nearly all his friends. He had tried to hide in the ship's hold, but an officer had found him and put him ashore again. No one wanted him anywhere. No ship would carry him. No country would let him land on its shores. Even the people of the country in which he was born shut the doors of their houses in his face. He was a good man and had money to pay his fare. Then why would no one take him? He was a leper.

Leprosy is a horrible disease. One who has it might better be

THE SAMARITAN PRAISED GOD AND FELL AT JESUS' FEET SO GRATEFUL WAS HE TO BE WELL

dead. People who have leprosy are called lepers, and there were many of them in Palestine when Jesus lived. No one else ever would touch a chair a leper had sat on or a dish he had used. Every time anyone passed, the lepers had to cry out "Unclean, unclean," for no one was allowed to go near them. They had to leave their friends and their homes. They had so little to eat I know they were often ill with hunger. A few filthy rags covered their poor suffering bodies. Can you imagine anything worse than being a leper?

In Palestine there were ten lepers who always kept close together. They wandered about the country, stopping near cities and little towns to beg. Never did they venture inside the city walls. When night came and the city gates were closed I suppose they crept into some caves among the rocks for shelter. These ten men had just heard some wonderful news. Some one had told them that a great Healer was traveling through the country, and that He could cure them. It was hard for the lepers to believe this, but a friend said that he had seen this Teacher raise the dead. Perhaps this friend had once been a leper himself and had been cured.

Every one of the ten was now watching for the Teacher. "He

surely will come our way some time," they must have thought. In the cheerless caves at night they all must have prayed that God would send the great Healer to them soon. There was one of them, at least, who surely prayed God to help him and to send Jesus the Healer to him. The poor fellow was a stranger, a Samaritan. The Jews hated these Samaritans. Would Jesus, who was a Jew, cure a Samaritan? Do you suppose the leper asked that question? No, I am sure he did not. Why? Because he knew that Jesus never asked who people were nor from where they came. Did they need His help? That was the question Jesus asked. Everyone who asked His help received it.

How eagerly the ten lepers must have watched every group of people that passed along the road to the city gate! And when Jesus and His disciples finally came, I can almost hear the call of the ten as they cried out: "Jesus, Master, have mercy on us!" And the Master heard their voices, although the lepers "stood afar off." They did not dare go near Him. Some stern soldier or pitiless Pharisee would have had them punished for coming too close to the throng of people around the city gate.

"Go and show yourselves unto the priests," Jesus answered them.

And off they went, hurrying to reach the priests. Not until a priest said that they were clean would they be allowed to come inside the city or to mingle again with their friends. As they ran, every man of them found that he was "clean," for the loathsome leprosy had been cured.

One turned back. He was the stranger, the Samaritan. God had heard his prayer and he was grateful. He would not go to the priests until he had thanked Jesus for his healing. Nine of Jesus' own people had passed on without a word. But this stranger praised God with a loud voice and fell at Jesus' feet, so grateful was he to be well again.

"Where are the nine?" Jesus asked him. "Among the ten that were healed," He added, "is only this stranger grateful?" He must have reached forth His hand and touched the man kneeling at His feet, as He said, "Arise, thy faith hath made thee whole."

The nine lepers ran on to visit the priests. They were glad to be well again, and that was all. When they came from the temple, what do you suppose they did? No doubt they ran to tell their friends of their wonderful cure. But what of the Samaritan stranger? I think he must have followed Jesus and learned from Him how to help others.

THE OTHER BROTHER

Ted lay curled up in a corner of the sofa. "Not outdoors this beautiful day?" asked his sister as she passed him. Ted's only answer was an impatient jerk of his shoulders. Everyone in the house was happy except Ted. He thought he had been badly treated and was cross.

"I think it's too mean for anything," he told his mother, "for Dad to give Walter that new pony. I'm older, I ought to have had it."

"Why, Teddy boy!" answered his mother, "we are all so happy because little brother can walk again and be strong like other boys that Dad gave him the pony just for joy."

THE OTHER BROTHER WHO LIVED IN PALESTINE

"Little Walter has been hobbling around on crutches in a hospital while you have been out playing," said Sister.

"Well, that was his own fault," answered Ted. "Mother told him not to go near that rickety platform, but he did, and he hurt himself."

"O Ted!" exclaimed Mother, "are you sorry that Walter is well and at home again?"

"I never had a pony," replied Ted, paying no attention to Mother's question. "Dad ought to have given it to me."

"You make me think of the other brother," said Mother.

"What other brother?" asked Ted.

"A boy that lived in Palestine many years ago, who was angry because his father gave his younger brother a present."

"Tell me about him," begged Ted.

"Some men who thought they were very good were angry with Jesus because He helped bad people just as quickly as He helped good people. So Jesus told a story to these people who thought they always did exactly right."

"Was it about the other brother?" asked Ted.

"Yes," answered Mother, "and you may tell me which of the two brothers in the story you like the better.

"The two brothers had everything they needed to make them happy, because their father was very rich. The younger brother must have been a jolly, lovable little fellow. Perhaps his father called him 'Sunshine' as he whistled cheerily around the house. He was a favorite with his playmates, for he was generous and shared his good things with them.

"But the other brother! No doubt he always obeyed his parents and his teachers, but he had a sour, surly way of speaking and acting, and he surely was stingy. I think he never shared his pleasures with anyone, and was afraid his father was not giving him all he deserved. I can hear him finding fault all the time and pointing out all that was bad in everything and everyone.

"When the boys grew to be men, their habits had not changed. The boy who loved people and a good time wanted to leave home. I am not surprised that he asked his father to give him his share of their wealth, and to let him go away and visit other countries.

"I am sorry to say, however, that this happy, generous young man was not wise. I think he enjoyed having people call him a 'good fellow.' It was easy for his friends to coax his money away from him. All they had to do was to flatter him. He

weakly yielded to them when they tempted him to do evil things. But he found listening to pleasant words from his wicked companions much more agreeable than listening to his brother's faultfinding at home.

"Yet money can't last forever, especially when one throws it away on foolish and wicked things as did this younger brother. When his money was gone, he could not buy any more rich gifts for his companions. Of course they deserted him as soon as he needed their help. He had no money to buy food, and he was in a strange country. Very often he was hungry. A farmer who kept many pigs needed a swineherd, and he was glad to find even this work. He need not starve, because

HE WASTED HIS MONEY WITH FOOLISH FRIENDS

73

he could eat some of the food that was given him to feed the pigs.

"I can see the young man standing in the midst of his herd of swine. His fine linen mantle and rich sandals are gone. He is ragged, cold, and oh, so dirty! He has no friends, for in that country everyone despises a swineherd. His only companions are those filthy pigs. He throws himself upon the ground with a bitter cry when he thinks of his father and his beautiful home. Not long does he lie there, however. Suddenly he jumps up and leaps over the wall of the swine yard. As he runs I can hear him shout, 'I'm going home to my father and tell him how foolish and wicked I have been! I had rather be at home as one of my father's servants than stay in this country.'

"But when he was still a long way from home his father met him. 'My dear, dear son!' his father cried. 'I have sorrowed because I thought you were dead, and now you have come back to me alive.'

"With arms about each other they walked home. Then the house was lighted with many lamps. The father gave a great party to welcome his son home. In silken robes and beautiful sandals the young man and his guests danced and enjoyed the rich feast and gay music.

"Then the father went out to tell the elder son the good news about his brother. What was the elder son doing? Sulking in a corner of the field, angry as he could be. 'I've stayed at home and worked and done right, but you never gave me a party for my friends,' he said to his father. 'Now as soon as this fellow who has wasted his money and done wickedly comes home you have a great feast for him.'

"I can hear the astonished father reply, 'Why, my son, you could have had a party any time. All that I have is yours to use whenever you want it. But your brother whom we thought dead is alive and at home again, and we should rejoice.'

"'Well, I shall not welcome him,' answered the other brother.

"The father returned to the house of joy and feasting, leaving his elder son alone and unhappy outside in the darkness."

Ted jumped from the sofa as he heard the clatter of hoofs approaching the house. He ran to the window just in time to wave his hand at the pale little fellow dashing past on his pony. What if Walter *had* been hurt because he was disobedient? Ted was glad that he was well again. "I'm not the other brother, Mother!" he shouted as he ran, toward the door.

RAGGED, HUNGRY, COLD AND LONELY, THE SWINEHERD STOOD THINKING LONGINGLY OF HIS OLD HOME

A CHILD'S PRAYER

Little Jesus, wast Thou shy
Once, and just so small as I?
And what did it feel like to be
Out of Heaven, and just like me?
I should think that I would cry
For my house all made of sky;
I would look about the air,
And wonder where my angels were.

Hadst Thou ever any toys
Like us little girls and boys?
Didst Thou kneel at night to pray,
And didst Thou join Thy hands, this way?
And did they tire, sometimes, being young?
And make the prayer seem very long?
And dost Thou like it best, that we
Should join our hands to pray to Thee?
(I used to think, before I knew,
The prayer not said unless we do.)
And did Thy Mother at the night
Kiss Thee, and fold the clothes in right?
And didst Thou feel quite good in bed,
Kissed, and sweet, and Thy prayers said?

Thou canst not have forgotten all
That it feels like to be small:
And Thou know'st I cannot pray
To Thee in my father's way—
Take me by the hand and walk,
And listen to my baby-talk.
To Thy Father show my prayer
(He will look, Thou art so fair),
And say: "O Father, I, Thy Son,
Bring the prayer of a little one."
And He will smile, that children's tongue
Has not changed since Thou wast young!

—ABRIDGED FROM FRANCIS THOMPSON

TWO LITTLE SONS

Little Christ was good, and lay
Sleeping, smiling in the hay;
Never made the cows' round eyes
Open wider at His cries;
Never when the night was dim,
Startled guardian Seraphim,
Who above Him in the beams
Kept their watch round His white
        dreams:
Let the rustling brown mice creep
Undisturbed about His sleep.

Yet if it had not been so —
Had He been like one I know,
Fought with little fumbling hands,
Kicked inside His swaddling bands,
Puckered wilful crimsoning face —
Mary Mother, full of grace,
At that little naughty thing,
Still had been a-worshiping.

—NANCY CAMPBELL

THE LITTLE SHEEP OF BETHLEHEM

The little sheep of Bethlehem
    Were not afraid that night,
When suddenly the gentle skies
    Grew strange with song, and bright;
When swift their shepherds went away
    And left them, small and still,
All huddled in a woolly heap
    Upon a lonely hill.
A peace was on the earth that night,
    Oh, very wide and deep;
Perhaps they knew they need not fear;
    Those blessed little sheep.

—ELIZABETH THORNTON TURNER

JESUS' LATER WORK

CHRIST BLESSING THE CHILDREN

THE MASTER'S BLESSING

Suppose we take another walk in Palestine. As we go we shall see many little children just big enough to toddle, others so tiny they must be carried. Along the country roads they come with their mothers. They are dressed in their best clothes, and their little faces and bodies no doubt have been rubbed with oil. The people in this country of Palestine think a rub with oil is much better than a dip in water.

Some timid mothers hang back as though afraid. Others walk so fast they have to drag their little children after them. Where are they all going? To see the Great Teacher, whom they lovingly call "Master."

"He surely will pass this way as He goes to Jerusalem," one mother says to another.

"But He may not look at our children," adds a quiet little woman.

"Jesus loves everyone. He surely must love little children," replies a happy mother as she hurries along with her four little ones.

Some of these women look sad. What can be the matter?

"My little girl was ill with a fever and Jesus healed her," says one.

"My husband waited one day by the mountain with our sick boy. None of the disciples could cure him, but Jesus did," adds a happy-looking woman.

"Everyone must love Him," many of them exclaim together.

"Not so," says a sad-faced woman. "Our rulers and the priests and Pharisees hate Him. I've been told they even plan to kill the Master when He reaches Jerusalem."

"Kill Jesus, the best friend we ever had! What has He done?" ask many shocked mothers.

"His disciples call Him the Christ, and once our people tried to seize Him and make Him king," a dark-eyed little woman answers.

Many of that group would like to have Jesus for their king, but every one of them knows that He does not care for palaces or crowns of gold. He wants to live among His people and make them happy.

If you and I keep on following this group of happy children we shall soon come to a village.

Ahead of us goes a Pharisee. Watch him stoop to shake the dust from his robe as a small boy runs past him. I can see by the frown on his face that he thinks children should stay at home and not be running around and kicking up dust on people's clothes.

"There! There! Don't you see the Master?" cries an excited mother.

A MOTHER BRINGING HER CHILDREN TO JESUS SO THAT HE MAY BLESS THEM

make a great deal of it. They seem unable to do anything quietly.

The disciples are angry. They do not wish Jesus to be interrupted. "What do you want here?" they ask the women. They seem cross and do not speak kindly.

"We have brought our children here for the Master to bless them," the mothers answer.

"What nonsense!" I can hear some of those disciples say. "Don't you know the Master is too busy to be bothered with children?"

See those poor, disappointed women turn to go away. Perhaps many of them have tramped with blistered feet along the dusty roads all day to get just one blessing for their babies. A simple prayer from the Master as He lays His hands on the curly heads was all the women asked. And the angry disciples have refused them this! I can see the women's eyes grow sad and their shoulders droop.

But only for a moment are they sad. They hear a voice telling them to stay, to bring their children to Him.

Jesus is calling them to bring the little ones to Him. I can see Him take the babies in His arms. Softly He strokes the heads of the small boys and girls who climb over Him as tiny tots the world

"Where is He? Where is Jesus?" eagerly asks another.

"Yes, but His disciples are all around Him. How can we get to Him?" asks a sad-faced woman.

"We must get to Him," they all agree. Many of these mothers and big sisters have walked many miles to bring the children to Jesus so that He may bless them. They look determined. I know they all will not willingly turn back until Jesus has laid His hands upon each little head.

Such noisy chattering the disciples hear as the group of children draws near! The people of Palestine seem to enjoy noise, for they always over will do with people who they know love them.

Around this little group stand the astonished disciples, the scornful rulers, and the sneering Pharisees. What! interrupt their wise words with Jesus just to please a lot of foolish mothers and their children! Of course they don't say such things aloud, but I can see by their faces that this is what they are thinking.

Jesus knows what they are thinking. I see Him rise with a chubby little child in His arms. He holds the little one out toward the people and says, "Let the little children come unto me, for the Kingdom of Heaven is like little children."

JESUS HOLDS THE LITTLE CHILD IN HIS ARMS

LAZARUS

A pretty path runs along the hillside. The small stones in it flash and sparkle as though they were laughing at the great gray rocks that rise above each side of the path. Gardens gay with flowers cover the hillside, and over their walls hang tree branches laden with delicious fruit. As you pass by, the trees seem to call out, "Come, pick my fruit, and eat." If you and I really were walking along that path the day on which our story begins, we'd surely answer, "Thank you, pretty trees, we'll gladly taste your fruit."

Thirteen men are slowly climbing the hillside along the path. Who are the men, and in what country is this hillside? They are Jesus and His apostles, and this is Galilee, the only place where the Master is safe from His enemies. All are talking earnestly together. Close to Jesus walk Peter, James, and John. I think Peter is saying to his brother Andrew, "How fortunate we were to escape from Judea!" The last time they were there the ungrateful Judeans had tried to stone the Master.

Judas shakes the moneybag which he carries. He probably is glad the Judeans did not try to steal his

JUDAS SHAKES THE MONEY BAG AND SO LONG
AS THAT IS SAFE HE IS HAPPY

gold. So long as that moneybag is safe, Judas is happy.

John and James are frowning as they follow Jesus. Neither of them can understand why the Master will not permit them to call down fire from heaven and burn to ashes His cruel enemies.

Following them up the path is another man. He seems in a great hurry to reach Jesus. I should think he might almost choke in the great cloud of dust he raises as he races along.

"I have a message for Jesus!" he shouts as he comes near.

Jesus stops when He hears the call and waits for the man. Panting and puffing from his long run the messenger makes known his errand.

"Lazarus, whom you love dearly, is ill, and his sisters have sent me to tell you."

Lazarus lives with his sisters, Martha and Mary, in Bethany of Judea. "Will Jesus dare go back to Judea?" question His apostles.

The messenger waits expectantly. Surely Jesus will go with him to Bethany. But no, Jesus bids him return alone while He and the apostles walk on to a small village among the hills.

Two days pass by. Then Jesus startles the twelve apostles by saying, "We must go back to Judea."

I can hear Peter anxiously trying to persuade Jesus not to return there. The other apostles all join Peter in urging the Master to keep away from the Judeans, who wish to kill Him.

"Lazarus is dead," Jesus tells them, "and I go to help him."

I can see all the apostles shake their heads as they wonder how it is possible to help Lazarus after he is dead. But they love their Teacher. So when they see that He is determined to go, they follow Him back into Judea.

Two days it takes to make the journey to Bethany. Martha is waiting for Jesus as He nears the pretty village. "You are too late," she tells Jesus. "My brother has been dead four days."

"Let me see where you have laid him," Jesus says. Then she and her sister Mary take Him to their brother's tomb.

There are many people crowding around the tomb. They are friends who have come to console Mary and Martha. The friends whisper among themselves. I can hear them asking one another, "If this man who opened the eyes of the blind loved Lazarus, then why did He let him die?"

Mary and Martha, thinking Jesus has come too late to help them, are weeping bitterly. The people are sorry for the sisters. They all feel that Jesus might have helped if only He had come sooner, but now it is too late.

But Jesus, too, is sorrowful. He stands for an instant with hands clasped and face uplifted in prayer. Then He walks quietly to the mouth of the tomb. A heavy stone rests against it.

"Roll the stone away!" Jesus commands the men who are standing near by.

Martha objects. Why open the grave when Lazarus has been dead four days? But willing hands roll away the stone. All are watching

LAZARUS HEARD JESUS' VOICE CALLING HIM AND CAME FORTH FROM THE TOMB

Jesus. Every voice is hushed. I believe that even the wind stopped playing with the leaves so that they should not rustle. That the bee humming in the sunshine crept into the heart of a flower and was quiet. And that the little bird stopped its song to listen.

The voice of Jesus calling, "Lazarus, come forth!" broke the stillness. The young man in the silence of his tomb hears that loved voice and comes forth. He has been dead, and now he is alive and well.

Great is the rejoicing of Mary and Martha as they walk with their brother away from the empty tomb.

SONS OF THUNDER

"I want to be first. I won't play unless I can be first," declared a shrill voice under my window, where some children were playing.

"I'm the eldest, I ought to be first," shouted a boy as he placed himself at the head of the line.

"I believe those little folks are playing soldier," I thought, as I looked out upon them. I was right. They were playing soldier, and each one wanted to be captain.

"I'm the biggest, I ought to be captain," the eldest boy told me.

"My father's a soldier, so I ought to be captain," chimed in a small girl.

Into my desk went pencils and paper. I thought it better to tell

these children a story than to write one for them. So I called to them saying, "If you'll stop quarreling, I'll come and tell you a story."

"We will, we will!" they shouted.

No captains are necessary when one is listening to a story. All that one needs is a pair of ears, and I could see that each one of my small listeners had a pair.

"What's the story about?" they asked, as we all seated ourselves on the grass.

"Two brothers, called 'Sons of Thunder,' who lived in Palestine with Jesus."

"Can thunder have sons?"

"No, of course not. When one is a son of thunder, it means he is brave, and often that he is warlike. John and James, disciples of Jesus, were very impatient and quick about everything they did. They often wanted to do things that angered the other disciples and that grieved Jesus. Like soldiers, the brothers wanted to kill all their enemies. Once they begged Jesus to command fire to come down from heaven and destroy a Samaritan village, because the people would not let Jesus and His disciples lodge there. Of course Jesus said 'No,' and rebuked the two angry brothers.

"It was a tiresome journey from Galilee to Jerusalem, especially so when one must walk all the way, as did Jesus and the disciples.

"On this journey Jesus had been telling them some wonderful news. All the disciples were greatly excited about it, especially James and John. Jesus had told them that He was soon to have a kingdom. What pleased the disciples most was to hear that each one of them was to have a throne all to himself and rule over part of the Hebrew people. All had left their homes to follow the Master. They wandered about the country with Him, often being driven from the cities and stoned. Do you wonder that when Jesus promised them thrones in His kingdom they were delighted? How

wonderful to be rulers, instead of being hunted like refugees!

"James and John told Salome, their mother, about it. I can hear her exclaim, 'My sons, you deserve the highest places in the Master's kingdom. I will go with you and we will ask Jesus for them.'

"The brothers nodded. They were as sure as their mother that the best places in the kingdom should be given to them. They forgot all about the other disciples, each one of whom no doubt was thinking that he himself deserved the highest honor.

"'Will you do something for us?' the brothers asked Jesus, as they, with their mother, came to the Master.

"'What do you wish?' answered Jesus.

"Up spoke Salome before her sons could answer. 'I want you to promise that you will give the best places in your kingdom to my sons. Let them sit next to you, one on your right, the other on your left.'

"What could Jesus reply? There were twelve disciples. No doubt each one wanted to sit on the right or left hand of Jesus, but none of them except James and John had dared ask Him for the honor.

"Then Jesus said, 'The places in My kingdom are not given away. Whoever wants a place there must earn it.' Then He added as He turned to the brothers, 'Are you able to work for what you want?'

"'Yes, we are willing and able,' replied the brothers.

"'Then you shall have the work to do,' Jesus told them.

"There the two brothers showed that they were true sons of thunder, for work did not frighten them. They did not whine because Jesus said He could not *give* them what they desired, but they must *earn* it.

"Did they win like real soldiers? Yes, for they learned that Jesus' kingdom did not mean golden thrones and purple robes, as the disciples thought at first. His kingdom which was to conquer and rule the whole world, was to be built up by

SALOME, THE MOTHER OF JAMES AND JOHN

JAMES AND JOHN SPENT THEIR LIVES IN
BLESSING OTHERS AND DOING KINDLY DEEDS

loving thoughts and kindly deeds. I wonder if Salome was satisfied!

"After Jesus left them to work alone, the two brothers spent their lives in blessing others. Never did John again ask to have fire consume his enemies. Instead he told them love was the law of the kingdom."

When my story was finished the eldest boy said, "That fellow next to you is a Boy Scout. Every day he does something to help somebody."

"He should be our captain," added the small girl whose father was a soldier.

"Let him have the first place," all the children exclaimed. "He deserves it."

AT THE HOUSE OF MARTHA

What do you suppose is happening in that large house on the hillside? From every direction people are hurrying toward it. A party? Yes, a great supper is being given by Mary and Martha in honor of Jesus. He and His disciples are on their way to Jerusalem to keep the Passover. They have stopped in Bethany of Judea, where Mary and Martha live.

Here come a number of scowling Pharisees. They have been invited to the supper, but are angry about it. Then why don't they stay at home? They are curious to see Martha's brother, Lazarus. Something very strange has happened to the young man, and they do not understand it.

Scribes in swishing silken garments are picking their way carefully along the road leading to Martha's house. How cross they all look — scribe, ruler, priest, and Pharisee! I should think they'd be ashamed to carry such sullen faces to a joyous supper party.

Other guests who seem glad and gay are coming. Big and little, rich and poor, all are anxious to see Lazarus. The Pharisees are bitterly angry, while the other people

"WE SURELY MUST GET RID OF THIS NAZARENE,"
SAID ONE PHARISEE TO ANOTHER

are joyfully happy over exactly the same thing. What can it be? Listen!

"We must put an end to the wonders this man Jesus is working," one Pharisee says to another.

The other replies, "All the people will be following Him if we do not stop them."

"Since Jesus raised Lazarus from the dead," a scribe remarks with a sneer, "more people are following Him every day."

"We must surely get rid of this Nazarene," they all agree.

"Why not kill Lazarus also?" some of them ask.

These wicked people are angry because Jesus is loved by those who

MARY POURING THE PRECIOUS OINTMENT OVER
THE HEAD OF JESUS

are ill, and by the poor and the unhappy. When Jesus raised Lazarus from the dead, Pharisee and priest decided to put an end to Him and to His wonderful works. From the hour in which they learned of that empty tomb or gazed spitefully after Lazarus walking through the town with his sisters, the Pharisees and priests began to plan some way in which they could destroy the Master. Why? Because the people would follow one who was kind to them and loved them. Jesus loved them and helped them in all their troubles.

Three months have passed since Jesus restored Lazarus to life. Mary and Martha are giving a supper to celebrate this wonderful event, and to honor the Friend who gave their brother back to them. All of their friends and many strangers have been invited. Mary and Martha must have thought, as they prepared for their guests, "All these people will see Lazarus and will believe in Jesus." And that is just what priest and ruler, scribe and Pharisee think, and that is the reason they are all so angry about the supper as they enter Martha's house.

The sun peeps through the lattice windows, and his golden light falls upon a long table around which the guests recline. Perhaps a mischievous sunbeam creeps into the eyes of a Pharisee and blinds him for a moment. But it does not matter. He would not believe what he saw anyway. So he may as well be blind.

The guests look with awe upon Lazarus. I can hear them talking among themselves and saying, "Can it be possible that this cheerful young man who is eating and drinking with us today once lay dead in his tomb?" When the eyes of the guests rest upon Jesus, who has done this, I know that some of them are thinking, "Surely this man Jesus must be the promised King."

Slowly the sun changes from gold to scarlet. His long red rays reach across the sky as though they were waving good night to the earth. The soft light falls upon the head of Jesus at the table. Who is the woman standing behind Him? It is Mary, Lazarus' younger sister. In her hand she has a beautiful flask filled with precious ointment. When she breaks it over the head of Jesus and pours the ointment upon His hair, the room is filled with fragrant perfume.

"What a waste of costly ointment!" some of the guests exclaim.

"Worse than that. It is money wickedly thrown away," declares Judas. "The ointment should have been sold and the money spent for the poor."

But the grateful heart of Mary pleases Jesus, and He smiles kindly upon her. "It was kind of her to do this for me," He tells the guests.

Honored guests very often were anointed with oil by their hosts. Oil was poured on the heads of kings when they were crowned. Among the people gathered round Martha's table are there only two who wish to do anything for Jesus? Is it only the sisters, Mary and Martha, who honor the One who has blessed them all? Perhaps Mary, as she stood behind Jesus and poured the ointment on His head, meant to say, "This is the King!"

BEHOLD YOUR KING!

The day awoke with a smile as the sun chased the night shadows out of its eyes. Sunbeams danced on leaf and flower and stole into people's houses bidding them be up and stirring. "Today is a happy, happy day," sang every bird and blossom and blade of grass.

When the sun said "Good morning!" at Martha's house, it must have found her with Mary and Lazarus, up and ready for a journey.

Today Jesus and His apostles start for Jerusalem to make ready for the Passover.

Down the road I can see a little band of people waiting for them.

MARY AND MARTHA WITH LAZARUS GOING TO JERUSALEM FOR THE PASSOVER

The eyes of all rest lovingly upon the One who is in the center of the group. It is Jesus, sitting upon an ass. "Now we are ready to start," shout many voices, and off they all walk toward Jerusalem.

Jesus, as He journeys, is joined by throngs of people. Like Himself, all are on their way to Jerusalem. Among the multitude that crowds about the Master I can see people who once were lame or palsied walking briskly along. A strong, well man greets a neighbor who does not turn away from him. A month ago no one would go near this same man because of his leprosy. Eyes are there that once were blind, but now see and enjoy the sunlight.

Rich and poor on camels and asses and on foot move in a great multitude toward the city. Now and then a Roman soldier on horseback, with shield and spear glittering in the sunshine, dashes past the long line of people. There are little children flitting in and out among the crowd like so many gay-colored butterflies. I can see a little boy and girl pull their mother's gown excitedly and hear them say to her, "Mother! Jesus smiled at us when we passed Him, just as He did the day He talked with the children!" The mother nodded happily. She, with many others, unfastened her outer cloak and threw it upon the roadway.

"The Master is coming this way," exclaimed a man as he flung his mantle across the road. He looked like a Samaritan. Perhaps he was the grateful leper healed by Jesus.

Lazarus casts his silken, gold-embroidered robe before the ass upon which Jesus sits. As he does so I hear him say to the multitude, "We do these things to honor kings, and so we do them for Jesus."

Slow progress can Jesus and His apostles make, for people from north, south, east, and west keep coming and crowding about Him. Many wave palm branches as they walk, while others strew leaves and flowers along His pathway. From grateful hearts springs a song of thanksgiving to their Friend and Helper.

Their shouts of joy are answered by the cries of another host of people coming toward them from Jerusalem. As they approach they cry, "Blessed is the King, the King of Israel!" Again the throngs with Jesus lift up their voices, shouting, "Blessed be the kingdom that is coming!"

In that joyous throng there are also scribes, Pharisees, priests, and rulers. They, too, are journeying to Jerusalem to keep the feast of the Passover. But not one word of

ONE MOTHER, UNFASTENING HER OUTER CLOAK, THREW IT IN THE PATHWAY OF THE MASTER

"JESUS A KING!" THE PEOPLE SNEER

praise do they speak. "Jesus a king!" I can hear them sneer. "A king wearing a golden crown who will make war and conquer our enemies is what we want!"

The shouts of the multitude anger these Pharisees so greatly that one of them rudely pushes through the crowd and reaches Jesus. "Do you hear what your disciples are saying?" he asks Jesus. He probably shakes his fist in the Master's face as he adds, "Tell your disciples to stop their shouts of praise!"

"The stones would give praise if the people did not," Jesus replies.

The faces of the apostles walking close to Jesus grow serious and sad.

They probably are thinking of the Pharisees who a few days before told Jesus to get out of the country because Herod wished to kill Him. I know they all are saying in their hearts, "It is not Herod, but the Pharisees and priests who would like to destroy the Master."

On the people move, until they come within sight of Jerusalem. Jesus halts. For a moment the host around Him is quiet. The beautiful Holy City lies before Him. In the midst of the city stands the temple, His Father's house He loves so dearly. Jesus does not smile. His eyes are filled with tears. He stretches out His arms toward the city as a mother stretches out her hand to her little one, and says, "Why will you destroy the friends who love you most? O Jerusalem! You know not how to have peace. Therefore your enemies shall destroy you."

Again the multitude moves on toward Jerusalem. They march to the walls of the city. The great gates are open wide to admit the pilgrims. Among them is the King. Through the archway He rides, but none recognize Him except His loving disciples and His apostles. "This man, say the people of Jerusalem, is the prophet Jesus from Nazareth of Galilee." But the disciples shout, "Behold your King!"

HOUSE OF PRAYER

When your mother buys meat for your dinner where does she get it? "At the market, of course," you answer. And if she wishes a pretty canary to sing in her window, she will go to the bird store for it. Butcher shops and bird stores are the proper places to buy beef and birds. You will be surprised when I tell you that once upon a time people sold animals in their churches. And the church I am going to tell you about, in which such things were done, was neither old nor useless, but new and very beautiful. From different countries, even from those far across the sea, people came to visit this wonderful church. You may have seen a picture of it, for it was the great temple in Jerusalem.

The temple was surrounded by a number of beautiful paved courts or yards. In these courts one could hear oxen lowing, sheep bleating, and doves cooing. They made so much noise I'm sure the priests inside the temple could hardly hear themselves speak when they taught the people.

Around the courts, were men sitting at small tables changing money. Piles of gold, silver, and copper coins lay on these little tables. The men at the tables were changing into Jewish coin, the money that strangers

MONEY CHANGERS IN THE COURTS OF THE TEMPLE

in Jerusalem had brought with them from their own country.

Into this beautiful temple came Jesus and His disciples. He loved the temple. It was God's house. He came there to pray and to teach. The sick and the poor, the lame and the blind followed Jesus always. They never gave their kind Friend any rest. Before the sun was up in the morning and late at night they kept coming to Him for help.

Through the temple courts passed Jesus and the people who followed Him. The noise and shouting of merchants buying and selling and making change must have made Jesus' face grow stern as He listened. No doubt the merchants looked at

Him and laughed. What did they care if the temple was God's house?

These men buying and selling in the temple knew that Jesus loved it. They knew He would use it only for healing and prayer. There they sat, impudently watching Jesus and His disciples. The eyes of these buyers and sellers as they looked at Jesus, must have said, "You can't stop us, even if you don't like what we are doing."

Did Jesus stop to ask whose task it was to take care of the temple courts? No, this beautiful temple was His Father's house. It had been built for prayer. God intended it as a shelter for all who were ill, poor, or unhappy. And these people whom God wanted to help were crowded out to make room for cattle and money changers!

Do you wonder that Jesus knotted a whip of strong cords and drove them all out of the temple? He must have opened the gates of the courts and turned the oxen and sheep into the valley. The dove cotes in the courts were torn down. To Jesus, His Father's house was not a place for cattle pens and dove cages.

Jesus overturned all the money tables. What a clattering there must have been as the gold and silver coins rolled out on the temple pavements! How the greedy eyes of publican and Pharisee must have glittered with hate as the coins rolled out of sight!

"You have made this temple a den of thieves instead of a house of prayer," said Jesus to the men who bought and sold in it. He would not stand quietly by while His Father's house was being wrongly used.

After these traders had been cast out of the courts, I can see Jesus and His disciples in the temple. There they will pray, and the sick people who followed Him will be cured.

While Jesus is blessing the people in the temple, very different things are happening outside. Pharisee and lawyer, priest and ruler are angry. They are planning to destroy Jesus and put an end to His work.

OUT OF HIS FATHER'S HOUSE JESUS DROVE ALL
THE TRADERS AND MONEY CHANGERS

A GREAT GIFT

Johnny had two shiny silver dimes which he jingled in his pocket as he walked to Sunday school. Uncle Nat had dropped them into Johnny's hand last night because for a whole week he had not mis-spelled a single word in his lesson. Those two dimes meant two picture shows or four ice-cream cones. Which should it be?

Before Johnny had decided, his cousin Mary ran up to him saying, "See Johnny! I have a whole nickel. Mother gave it to me for wiping the supper dishes last night."

"What you going to do with it?" asked Johnny.

"Buy five choc'late pep'mints," she answered. "I jus' love choc'late pep'mints."

Side by side the two children entered the Sunday-school room and sat quietly listening while their teacher told them about a far-away country where some poor little children were dying of hunger. Then a box was passed around, and all the children dropped money into it. Johnny watched one of his shiny silver dimes slip through the slit into the box. How fine it made him feel to be giving ten pennies to help buy food for starving children! He thrust his hand into his pocket and felt of the dime that was left. He nodded his head cheerfully as he thought, "I've still something left for myself."

Mary, almost ashamed that she had so little to give, slipped her nickel into the box. Then her pocket was empty.

Dear little girl and dear little boy! They did not know it, but by their acts they really were telling a Bible story. I'm sure you would like to hear the Bible story which Johnny and Mary acted without knowing it.

Now we'll pretend that we are at the temple in Jerusalem. We are walking in a great hall whose roof rests upon pillars so large that several pairs of short arms like yours would be needed to reach around one of them. Some of these pillars

IN THE GREAT HALL OF THE TEMPLE IN JERUSALEM

THE PHARISEE AND THE POOR WIDOW DROPPING OFFERINGS IN THE TREASURY BOXES OF THE TEMPLE

have great boxes fastened to them. What are these boxes for? Wait a moment and watch closely.

There comes a Pharisee. He pulls a bag from his bosom and takes out a handful of money and into one of the boxes lets fall some jingling gold pieces. Each box is labeled. The box into which the Pharisee dropped his money is labeled, "For the poor." "How generous that Pharisee must be!" you are thinking. Yes, but in the bag in his bosom is twice as much money as he slipped into the treasury box.

We hear a swishing of silken garments and looking around see a scribe approach a box and put in more gold. He watches to see how many people noticed his large gift and praised him for his generosity. The scribes and Pharisees want everybody to know how wealthy and generous they are. Some even have a bell rung just before they say their public prayers or give alms.

Jesus is in the temple, sitting close to the treasury boxes. Peter, Judas, and the other apostles are with Him. Judas, I am sure, takes his bag of money out of his bosom and wonders when it will be as full and heavy as the bags of those two rich rulers coming through the temple courts. Peter, I know, is wondering why Jesus stays on in Jerusalem when the rulers, scribes, and Pharisees are planning to kill Him. "Jesus," Peter thinks, "would be much safer in Galilee."

Hark! A baby is crying! Yes, it is snuggled close in its mother's arms, as she walks timidly toward one of the treasury boxes, the one with the label, "For the temple." But where is her money bag? She has none. She is a poor widow who loves the temple and wants to put something into its treasury. A single copper coin in her fingers is all the money she has. She worked hard for it, although it is worth less than one of our pennies. With a happy smile she slips her bit of money into the box, then turns and goes quickly out of the temple.

Judas and the other disciples are praising the people who have given much, although they still have left a great deal more than they gave. But Jesus does not praise the scribes and Pharisees who gave large sums of gold. He says that the greatest gift put into the treasury that afternoon was the widow's mite—that simple copper coin—*all she had*. She has given all her living and must work hard if she needs more money. I can see Judas frown. He does not like to have the woman praised when she gave so little.

You and I know why Jesus praised her. She cheerfully gave all that she had. And now you know how it was that Johnny and Mary acted a Bible story without knowing it.

A SAD SUPPER

Did your mother ever tell you to sit up straight at the table and not get under it by slipping down in your chair? I'm almost sure she did. Mine did when I was a little girl. In Palestine people didn't like to sit up when they ate. They drew wide couches close to their low table and lay down on them. They were careful, though, to have their heads and hands next to the table.

Tonight I want you to go with me to a supper in Palestine. There will be no little girls or boys there. We shall see thirteen men only. All of them are looking sad as they recline at the table. No, I am mistaken, one of them does not look sad. That man even seems happy as he carelessly jingles some silver pieces which lie in the bag he carries.

These thirteen men are Jesus and His twelve apostles. The apostles are sad because Jesus has told them that this is the last supper they will ever eat together.

"Tonight I am going to be taken away from you by wicked men who will kill me," Jesus said.

"But we are here," the apostles must have answered. "We will not let the priests and the Pharisees find you. If they do not find you they cannot hurt you."

Jesus' face, always full of love for everyone, tonight was white and sad. He seemed to be suffering as He answered the apostles, "One of my own friends who is eating with me at this table is going to show the priests and Pharisees where they may find me and how to seize me."

"One of us!" the shocked apostles all answered. Even the apostle with the moneybag shook his head as if he could not believe it. Then each one of them anxiously asked, "Lord, is it I?"

"It is one of you at the table," Jesus replied. The apostle with the bag seemed uneasy. No doubt

JESUS TELLING HIS APOSTLES THAT THIS IS THE LAST SUPPER THEY WILL EVER EAT TOGETHER

he was afraid to raise his eyes and look at Jesus.

Sad as was this supper, and sorry as were all of them that Jesus was going to be taken away from them, the apostles began to dispute together. And what do you think the dispute was about? They were quarreling over which one of them was going to be the most important. Each one of them was sure *he* ought to be greatest. Jesus did not *say* anything but He *did* something. He quietly rose from the table, put some water in a basin, and wrapped a towel around His waist. Then He washed the

JESUS WASHING THE FEET OF ONE OF THE APOSTLES

98

feet of His twelve apostles. Were their feet dirty? Certainly not. In Palestine washing a person's feet meant that you loved him and wanted to do something for him.

"Why do you wash our feet?" asked Peter.

"Because I want to show you that you are not helping any one by quarreling about who shall be first," replied Jesus. "I came into the world to help people, and that is the only reason you are in the world, just to help—that is, to serve—all people who need it."

I believe all the apostles except Judas were ashamed that they had quarreled. But Judas carried the bag with the money in it, and he was sure that the most important of them all was the man with the money.

When Jesus came back to the table He dipped a piece of bread in some oil and handed it to Judas. "Do quickly what you are going to do," He said to him.

Up jumped Judas from the table and hurried away. Probably the other apostles wondered why Judas didn't wait and go with them to the garden, for he always had gone with them. Judas did intend to go to the garden of Gethsemane that same night, but not with Jesus and the apostles.

THIRTY PIECES OF SILVER

How many little folks have bags in which they keep their pennies? And how often those pennies are poured out on the table just to be counted! Judas, one of Jesus' apostles, always carried a bag of money. Whenever Jesus or any of His apostles needed anything, they always sent Judas out to buy it. Judas was their banker. A heavy bag meant one with lots of money in it. A heavy bag made Judas happy, because he loved money.

Watch him stalking along the road angrily swinging his bag back and forth! He is angry with Jesus.

JUDAS, ANGRY WITH JESUS HURRIES TO THE GARDEN

JUDAS STRETCHED FORTH HIS HANDS GREEDILY, AND THE PRIEST PUT INTO THEM THIRTY SHINY SILVER PIECES

Yesterday Jesus overturned the money tables in the temple and the money rolled away and was lost. "Some of that money should be in my bag," thought Judas. "My bag should be full, not nearly empty," he tells a Pharisee walking beside him.

"Why?" asked the Pharisee.

"Because day before yesterday Jesus let a woman empty a whole box of expensive ointment on His head. He should have told her to sell it and give Him the money," Judas answered.

"But it wouldn't have been your money," said the Pharisee.

"No, but it would have been in my bag, for Jesus and His disciples give me all their money to carry," answered Judas.

The chief priests are glad that Judas is angry with Jesus. Perhaps he will listen to them if they offer him money. So they call to him and he stops to talk with them. "I don't want to be giving things to people all the time, the way Jesus does. I want to get something for myself," I can hear Judas tell the wicked men who hate Jesus.

"Will you help us to arrest Jesus?" the chief priests ask.

"I will if you pay me enough for it," Judas answers. Then Judas stretched forth his hands greedily, and the priests put into them thirty shiny silver pieces.

Judas is happy, for now his bag is heavy. He thinks he has fooled the priests and Pharisees, for Judas feels sure these wicked men cannot hurt Jesus. He remembers the time Jesus fed five thousand people with only two fishes and five loaves of bread. He thinks of the time Jesus walked on the water and quieted the wind by just speaking to it, and he remembers when He brought Lazarus up out of his tomb. "If Jesus can do all these things He can save Himself," Judas no doubt thought.

"Wait until night comes, then I will lead you to Gethsemane," Judas told the priests and rulers. "Jesus will be there alone with His apostles and it will be easy for you to take Him," he added.

"How are we going to know Jesus in the dark?" the Pharisees asked Judas.

"Arrest the person I kiss," Judas answered.

The sun slipped away from the earth. The moon came up over the hills and showered silver moon-beams over everything.

But the silver in the bag was the only kind of silver for which Judas cared. For those silver pieces he had sold Jesus to the men who meant to kill Him. I'm sure that night the rulers, the mob, and Judas skulked in the shadows of trees and rocks as they walked to the garden.

Judas opened the garden gate and greeted Jesus with a kiss. The mob seized Jesus and led Him away. Instead of trying to get away, as Judas expected, Jesus allowed the brutal mob to beat and abuse Him.

Judas waited until Jesus was condemned to death. "Why doesn't He save Himself? I did not think they could hurt Jesus," he must have kept muttering to himself, and I am sure he added, "I sold Him for thirty pieces of silver, but I thought He could get away."

When morning came Judas took his bag and went to see the priests and rulers. Inside out he turned the bag, and the silver pieces fell jingling at the feet of the priests. "I do not want your money," he told them. "I was wicked to take it. Jesus never has done any wrong."

"We don't care about that," replied the rulers. "We hate Him and we are going to kill Him."

Miserable, unhappy Judas! How he hated those thirty pieces of silver now! And he must have hated himself, too, for he went out and hanged himself.

THE FRIEND WHO WAS AFRAID

The moon was playing hide and seek with the clouds. First one little cloud and then another darted a fleecy finger into the moon's face. But the moon would not stay hidden. It sailed so fast and so high it left the saucy clouds behind, and made the stars stop twinkling and disappear.

High in the heavens the moon smiled down upon a beautiful garden filled with olive trees, and threw a shower of silvery moonbeams over a man kneeling in the garden. The man was Jesus. But He was not alone. If you had looked closely you would have seen the disciples

JESUS AT PRAYER IN THE GARDEN OF GETHSEMANE

off by themselves asleep under the olive trees.

Jesus had asked His disciples to watch with Him in this garden called Gethsemane. "We surely will," all of them answered, and Peter had added, "You say that wicked men are coming tonight to take you away from us, and that they will kill you. But I will not let them." And the rest of the disciples had said, "We will all stay with you and help you."

Jesus had smiled very sadly, as He answered, "You think now that you love me, but tonight all of you are going to run away and leave me."

"Not I," said Peter. "The others may run away, but I shall stay with you even though the priests and the Pharisees put me in prison and kill me."

What fine, brave words! But they did not make Jesus happy. He looked at Peter as though He felt sorry for him and said, "This very night, Peter, before the cock crows, you will have denied three times that you know me."

"Never!" replied Peter. "I am ready to die for you." Perhaps Peter was saying to himself, "When the cock crows! Why, it is now nearly midnight. I can't forget Jesus in just a few hours."

A dark cloud crept slowly toward the moon and threw a black veil

THROUGH THE GATE CAME A MOB OF ANGRY MEN

over its face. Jesus rose from the ground and wakened His disciples. They had forgotten that they came to the garden to watch with Him. Jumping up, the disciples saw, coming through the garden gate, a mob of angry men carrying lanterns, clubs, and swords. When some of them seized Jesus roughly and tried to tie His hands together, Peter bravely drew his sword and cut off the ear of the high priest's servant.

"Put up your sword," Jesus said to Peter.

Then what do you think Jesus did? He stretched forth His bound hands and healed the bleeding ear. Jesus always did kind deeds, even to the people who abused Him.

Then off to the high priest's house the mob carried Jesus. If He had looked around He would have seen only people who hated Him—the scribes, the proud Pharisees, and the rulers. Of those disciples who had promised to stay with Him, all but one had run away, just as Jesus had said they would. Where was Peter? Surely he did not run away! No, you can see him following the mob, but he is so far behind that none of the mob can see him. He skulks along in the shadow of the rocks and trees.

Jesus, tired and cold, was hurried into the high priest's house. No one offered Him a seat or asked Him to come near the fire. He had to

JESUS IN THE HOUSE OF THE HIGH PRIEST

"I DO NOT KNOW THE MAN OF WHOM YOU SPEAK," SAID PETER

stand while the horrible mob spat upon Him, struck Him in the face, and tore His clothing nearly off.

Peter sat comfortably by the fire warming his hands. He must have wondered why Jesus did not fight His enemies, and said to himself, "Jesus has the power to destroy these wicked people. Why doesn't He do it and save Himself?" Do you suppose Peter began to doubt the power of Jesus because He would not strike back? I fear so. Poor Peter! He was so badly frightened he forgot Jesus had told His disciples, that after He was crucified and buried, He should rise from the tomb and see and talk with them again.

A young maiden pointed at Peter and said, "You are a disciple of this Nazarene, Jesus."

"I am not. I don't even know whom you are talking about," Peter replied angrily. Then see him try to slip out of the room! But it was useless.

A man met Peter at the door and said, "I saw you in the garden tonight with Jesus."

Peter was so angry he wanted to strike the man. "You did not, for I was not there. I do not know the man of whom you speak," he said, pushing his way through the door.

Outside there was a maid watching. She, too, called to Peter, "You are a disciple of Jesus."

Peter must have clenched his fists as he replied, "I tell you I do not know this Jesus."

As he spoke, the long, shrill call of the cock rang out. It was three o'clock in the morning and three times Peter had denied knowing the Master. Peter heard and remembered what Jesus had told him. Don't you suppose he clapped his hands over his ears to shut out the sound and rushed into the darkness?

The moon had slipped from the sky. There was nothing to see but a chilly mist. Peter shivered, but not with fear. He was ashamed of himself, and oh, so sorry!

CALVARY

The day was dark and gloomy. The sun had hid his face as if ashamed to shine, and I do not wonder. Even a ball of fire like our sun would try not to look upon the awful things that were happening in Jerusalem that day.

Along a narrow street came a procession. No, it was not a procession, but a howling, shrieking mob. Men were hurling ugly words and stones at a prisoner who was being led through the city gates. The prisoner was Jesus. Many weeping women were following the mob. Some of these women spoke kindly to the prisoner. Perhaps they offered Him a cup of cold water, or a cloth with which He could wipe His blood-stained face. No doubt these faithful women were roughly torn away from Jesus by priest and scribe, who in their fury savagely threw them to the ground.

Jesus had broken no laws. He loved people and had been kind to them. He healed them when they were ill. He made blind eyes see, lame feet walk, and sorrowful people happy again. Even sinners were different people after they had talked with Jesus. He always made it seem easier to be good than to be wicked. But priest, scribe, Pharisee, and

THE MOB WITH JESUS IN THEIR MIDST MOVED SLOWLY THROUGH THE CITY GATES

governor wanted to kill Jesus. Why did they want to kill Him? Because the people loved Him and called Him "King" and "Christ."

"We will not have that kind of king," the rulers said.

They wanted fine palaces, big armies, and kings that conquered their enemies by wicked wars. Jesus taught how to rule by love, and therefore priest and ruler hated Him. People who have hate and anger in their hearts forget how to love. That was the trouble with the priests and rulers. They had hated their enemies for so long that I believe if you could have taken out their hearts and looked at them, you would have found them black with hate and hard as stone.

On moved the procession until it was outside the walls of Jerusalem. Across the shoulders of Jesus lay a cross. It was large, and much too heavy for Him to carry. He bent low to the ground under the burden. Finally Jesus stumbled and fell. Then the soldiers stopped a man who was passing and made him bear the cross.

The soldiers had placed a crown of thorns upon Jesus' head. His forehead was covered with scratches, and His back was bleeding from the lashes of stout whips. But scribe and Pharisee, priest and ruler laughed aloud as they saw His suffering. The man they hated was to be crucified, and they were glad.

Pilate, the governor, had wanted to set Jesus free. "He has done nothing wrong," Pilate said.

But the ignorant people, led by their savage rulers, had shouted, "Crucify Him! Crucify Him!"

"But Jesus is king of the Jews," many people had said.

"Not so," shouted scribe and Pharisee. "We have no king but Caesar."

So Jesus was given to the men who hated Him. This dreadful band of cruel rulers was allowed to destroy the best Friend the people ever had. Outside the walls of the city, then on toward Golgotha, the procession went. The cross was thrown upon the ground and Jesus was stretched upon it. After they had fastened Him to the cross, they raised it to let Him hang there by His hands until He died.

The hands of Jesus that had blessed little children, that had fed the hungry, that had lovingly touched the loathsome leper, and had made the blind to see, now were bleeding from the sharp nails which fastened them to the cross. The feet that always had hurried to the side of those who needed His help were torn by a great spike which had been driven through them.

On the cross above Jesus' head was the title, "Jesus of Nazareth, the King of the Jews." Pilate had written it and had it placed there.

All morning the sun had been hiding. The clouds had been growing blacker and blacker until by noon it was dark as night. Not a leaf moved, not a bird sang. When men act like savages and wild beasts, it is not surprising that strange things happen. "Hate must be our king, we will not have love," the rulers said in their hearts. And so the One who loved them best they crucified.

THE PROCESSION MOVING SLOWLY ON ITS WAY TO GOLGOTHA

THE MASTER

"The Master has come over Jordan,"
  Said Hannah, the mother, one day;
"He is healing the people who throng Him,
  With a touch of His finger, they say.
And now I shall carry the children,
  Little Rachel and Samuel and John,
I shall carry the baby Esther,
  For the Lord to look upon."

The father looked at her kindly,
  But he shook his head and smiled,
"Now, who but a doting mother
  Would think of a thing so wild?"
. . . .
"Nay, do not hinder me, Nathan,
  I feel such a burden of care,
If I carry it to the Master,
  Perhaps I shall leave it there.
If He lay His hand on the children,
  My heart will be lighter, I know,
For a blessing for ever and ever
  Will follow them as they go."

So over the hills of Judah,
  Along by the vine-rows green,
With Esther asleep on her bosom,
  And Rachel her brothers between;
'Mong people who hung on His teaching,
  Or waited His touch and His word,
Through rows of proud Pharisees list'ning,
  She passed to the feet of our Lord.

"Now, why shouldst thou hinder the
    Master,"
  Said Peter, "with children like these?"
. . . .
Then Christ said, "Forbid not the children;
  Permit them to come unto Me";
And He took in His arms little Esther,
  And Rachel He sat on His knee.

And the heavy heart of the mother
  Was lifted all earth-care above,
As He laid His hands on the brothers,
  And blessed them with tenderest love;
As He said of the babes in His bosom,
  "Of such is the Kingdom of Heaven."
And strength for all duty and trial
  That hour to her spirit was given.
                              —JULIA GILL

THE NAZARENE

He told us everything he could
  About the lilies, and the way
The shepherds carry home the lambs
  Within their arms at close of day;
How we within our Shepherd's fold
  Are ever safely housed and fed,
And all who walk with tender Love
  Like little lambs are gently led.

E'en as a hen beneath her wings
  Shelters her tiny trembling brood,
He would have gathered in his arms
  The world had they but understood.
He spoke to all the humble folk
  And told them just such lovely
      things,—
Of how the Father guards and guides
  Even the sparrow's drooping wings.

He told them of a son who left
  His home and wandered hungering,
And who on turning back had met
  Such joy and happy welcoming.
He told them Love is ever Love,
  And falls on all like gentle rain;
He told them everything he could,
  Then turned and blessed, and blessed
      again.
                    —MARION SUSAN CAMPBELL

SPREADING THE GOOD NEWS

THE WOMEN WHO CAME TO THE TOMB WITH FLASKS OF OINTMENT AND BOXES OF SPICES
FOUND IT OPEN AND EMPTY

WHEN THE PROMISE WAS KEPT

Who is up first in the morning? The birds, of course. Long before our sleepy eyes are open, the birds are flitting about in our gardens and calling to one another.

One morning long, long ago, so early that only the birds were awake, some women were walking up a stony path toward a garden. Each one of them carried a flask of ointment or a box of costly spices. In that garden someone they loved was buried, not in the earth, but in a rocky cave. These women had sad faces because Jesus, their friend, lay in that tomb. They had watched when He had been laid in it, and they knew exactly where to find it in the garden.

"But how are we to get into the tomb to leave our spices?" one woman asked.

"A great stone closes the opening," another said.

"Yes," they all added, "and the chief priests and the Pharisees have set a guard of soldiers around it!"

Those silly priests and foolish Pharisees! As if a guard of soldiers and a heavy stone sealed tight could keep Jesus in the tomb! The priests and Pharisees themselves were afraid they could not keep Him there.

Why? Because, only a few days before His death, Jesus had told them that, even if they killed Him, in three days He would rise again out of His tomb.

On the women toiled up the steep, stony path, all of them wondering how they could get past the guard of soldiers and who would roll away the great stone from the door of the tomb. Soon they came to the garden. How quiet everything was! Not a sound except the happy song of a little bird, glad that the morning was so near. The gray mist was beginning to disappear behind pink clouds. The wind was whispering merrily to the leaves that danced and rustled as if it were saying "good morning" to them.

The women stood still. On each face was a look of astonishment. Not a soldier was in sight. Some swords may have been lying on the ground, perhaps a helmet or even a shield had been dropped.

"The soldiers who were here must have left in a hurry," the women probably were thinking. What had frightened these stern men?

The women moved on toward the tomb. Their tear-dimmed eyes opened wide. Perhaps they dropped their boxes of spices, so surprised were they. Now they knew what had frightened the soldiers away.

"JESUS IS NOT DEAD, HE HAS RISEN FROM THE TOMB!"

The tomb was wide open. The heavy stone had been rolled away and the strong seal which had fastened it to the opening of the cave was broken. They stooped down and looked inside the tomb. It was empty. No, there in the darkness stood someone whose face shone like a wonderful light. The women thought him an angel. He spoke to them saying, "Why do you come here to find Jesus? He is alive and is risen, just as He told you."

Jesus had told His disciples and the people that He was going to live, and because He lived, they should live. His words were true. His promise had been kept. He had shown them all that no wicked thing or person could kill Him.

"Go tell the disciples that He is alive," said the stranger with the shining face.

Down the steep hillside flew the happy women. They ran until they reached Jerusalem and the house in which the disciples sat.

"The tomb is empty! Jesus is not dead, He has risen!" the women joyously exclaimed. But the disciples would not believe them.

Out in the country, a long way from the garden and its tomb, two sorrowing men were walking. It was now afternoon. The sun had never seemed more golden. Lambs and frisky kids frolicked in the fields. Even surly camels must have had a twinkle in their eyes as they passed the men. But these two travelers never noticed how happy everything seemed to be, because their own thoughts were so sad and gloomy.

"This is the third day," said one of the men, "and as yet nothing has happened."

The other spoke, saying, "Jesus told us He would rise on the third day, and now it is late in the afternoon." Both shook their heads in sorrowful disappointment. A third man, a Stranger, joined them. To Him the two travelers began to tell their grief.

"Jesus of Nazareth, a great prophet, was crucified last Friday. We had hoped He was the one who would save Israel," the two travelers told this Stranger who had joined them.

As the men talked, their hearts grew lighter. Perhaps they began to notice how lovely the day was, and to be cheered by the gay-colored flowers along the roadside. The Stranger had wonderful eyes. They seemed to see the thoughts in the men's minds. And His smile was kind and loving. How did it happen that He had not heard of the cruel act on Calvary?

The two men listened as the Stranger talked to them about the Scriptures. Then as He spoke about Christ, slowly that awful picture of Calvary disappeared, and they saw a tomb open, and the Master they loved walk forth.

"Why didn't we recognize Him while He was talking to us and know that He was Jesus?" the two men asked after the Stranger had left them. Like the women, they also ran to tell the disciples not to grieve any more, for Jesus was alive.

And what about those disciples who would not believe? With all these witnesses they still doubted that Jesus lived. Why is it so hard for people to believe good news? Then one day Jesus came to them as they sat together in a room. He showed them His hands and His feet pierced and torn by the nails which had fastened Him to the cross. "I am alive," Jesus told them. And at last the disciples believed.

They were no longer sad. Every one of them now wanted to go out and tell the people everywhere that Christ had overcome death.

Then one sunny day as they stood together on a hillside, a cloud came up and hid the Master. When the cloud passed, the disciples were alone. Now, what He had taught them was living in their hearts.

When Jesus left them His disciples must have remembered what He once had told them: that the will of God is that man should live forever.

ONE SUNNY DAY A CLOUD CAME UP AND HID THE MASTER. THEN THE DISCIPLES WERE ALONE

113

BREAKFAST BY THE SEA

Very early in the morning, so early that the day had not changed its raiment of misty gray for its gay sunny robe, seven men were fishing in the Sea of Galilee. All night they had been out in their boats and not a single fish had come near their net. No wonder they were tired and discouraged! They probably were cold also, for morning fogs do not make warm wraps.

Jesus had done many wonderful things in Galilee. The seven fishermen out on the sea had seen those wonders, for they were Jesus' apostles. "And now everything has ended," they must have been thinking. "Cruel men have crucified the Master, and He has been laid in the tomb." To be sure, the tomb was empty and Jesus had risen, but He was not there with them as He used to be, and they could not understand it.

"Let us go fishing," Peter had said, and the seven apostles had started to the Sea of Galilee. Good fishermen though they all were, not one among them had been able to catch even a single fish during the long night.

"We might as well go ashore. There's nothing here for us," I can hear some of them say. I know each one of them was saying in his heart, "Oh, if only Jesus were here!"

Much to their surprise, they saw someone over on the shore waiting for them. "Who can it be?" they asked one another. Perhaps they feared some Roman soldier was watching for them, or that a scribe was waiting to arrest them because they had been with Jesus. A scribe had no right to arrest them, but many things had been done in these last few days that no one had a right to do. Jesus had been wickedly put to death. The apostles did not expect any better treatment from the rulers than their Master had received.

Slowly they approached the shore. Hark! A voice they love is calling to them.

"Have you anything to eat?" it asked.

"Not a thing," was the disciples' answer. "We have fished all night and caught nothing."

"Your net is on the wrong side of the boat," replied the voice on the shore. "Throw it over on the right side and you will find plenty of fish."

On the other side of the boat the net was thrown. Down, down into the sea it sank. I think it must almost have pulled the apostles

THE NET NEARLY BROKE, SO HEAVY WAS IT WITH FISH

in after it, for the net nearly broke, so heavy was it with fish. The apostles gazed wonderingly at one another. All began to suspect that the figure waiting for them on the beach was Jesus.

"It is the Master," whispered John to Peter. Eagerly the apostles pushed the boat forward, dragging after them the great net filled with fish. But Peter could not wait for the boat to land. Hastily he tied on his outer coat and cast himself into the sea. His strong limbs could carry him ashore much quicker than the boat.

At last all were together on the shore. Jesus had everything ready for them. He knew they must feel chilly after that long, lonely night on the water, so He had a fine fire of burning coals waiting for them. Breakfast was ready, also. Bread and broiled fish. How happy those apostles must have been as they sat around the fire on the beach talking with Jesus! He had been cruelly crucified, but had come back to them as He had promised.

I can see the golden sunshine of the morning creep across the dark sea and make every wave

"I HAVE TAUGHT YOU TO BE FISHERS OF MEN,"
JESUS SAID TO THE APOSTLES

sparkle in the light. But the dancing waters shone no brighter than
the happy faces of the apostles as
they listened to Jesus.

"I have taught you to be fishers
of men," He said. "I cannot stay
with you much longer, but I expect
you to go out into all the world and
teach people everywhere what I have
taught you, and do the wondrous
works that I have shown you how
to do."

Many people are gathered on the
seashore and gaze in wonder on
the Master risen from His tomb.
Some follow Jesus and His apostles
as they walk toward a hill near
Bethany. Lazarus with Mary and
Martha may meet Him there and
give Him a joyous greeting. The
cruel cross, the dark tomb no longer
cause them sorrow. Jesus has overcome them. They could not hurt
Him. He has promised His disciples the same power. Will they
use it?

Slowly the Master climbs the
rough, steep hillside. The people
remain behind. Only eleven apostles are following now. Seven ate
with Jesus on the seashore. The
other four joined the happy group
as they journeyed toward Bethany.

Jesus is far ahead. He has reached
the top. He turns to bless the
eleven. Upon His face I know there
rested a holy smile of tenderness
for His "friends," as He called the
apostles. They lifted their eyes to
look upon Him. The light is brilliant. For a moment it dazzles them.
Then slowly across the mountain
top a fleecy cloud floats between the
apostles and Jesus. He is hidden
from their sight.

The cloud passes by and is gone.
The apostles look again at the spot
where Jesus stood, but He is not
there. They know in their hearts
that He has left them and now they
must do their work alone. They
can do it, for the Master has shown
them the way.

MANY TONGUES

Was it evening or was it morning when the apostles said good-by to Jesus on the hillside? I like to think it was nearing twilight, when the clouds were beginning to put on their pretty gay-colored dresses just before the sun slipped out of sight behind the hills. From red to pink, from gold to green and then to pale gray, the clouds changed. A bright star shone in the sky, and a mist crept slowly up from the valley. Not until a moonbeam told the people that night had come did any one of them turn away and go to their homes in Jerusalem. Every one of the disciples, the women who followed Jesus, and perhaps some little children He had blessed stumbled down the darkening path toward the lights of the city.

"We shall have to do our own work now," some apostles must have said. Perhaps a few were ashamed because they had been selfish and had asked Jesus to do their work instead of doing it themselves. Do you know any girls or boys who are like these apostles, always asking mother or teacher to do their hard work for them? Sometimes small fingers are lazy ones.

Quietly through the noisy streets of Jerusalem the apostles walked.

They must have met scowling scribes and tricky Pharisees who mocked them, saying, "We have killed their master, we shall hear no more from them." The chief priests talking on the street corners no doubt were planning to turn out of the synagogue everyone who loved Jesus. "This band of ignorant people won't disturb us again," the chief priests and scribes probably said.

The apostles and Jesus' other friends kept together. A house in Jerusalem sheltered them from their enemies, who meant to kill them if ever they mentioned the name of Jesus. For ten days and nights this little group of people remained together and prayed. They were so

THE ENEMIES OF JESUS ARE PLANNING TO KILL
HIS APOSTLES

117

quiet no one knew they were praying. The people outside liked noisy prayers. They thought the more noise one made the better one prayed.

At last, early one morning, all the apostles heard a sound like that made by a strong, rushing wind, and then upon the head of each apostle there rested a light, brilliant and beautiful. No one but the apostles saw the light. But soon everyone in Jerusalem knew about it, because all those upon whom the light shone were able to speak many tongues — that means they were able to speak and understand different languages. Every lonely stranger in Jerusalem heard the language of his own country spoken by the apostles.

UPON THE HEAD OF EACH APOSTLE RESTED A LIGHT

"These men from Galilee never have been to our schools. Then how can they speak so many different languages?" priests and scribes must have asked.

Do you suppose that the people who thought they had killed Jesus were frightened when they heard the apostles talking? I am sure they were. Instead of a few people in Palestine hearing about Jesus, now the whole world was going to know of Him. Rich rulers and Pharisees thought they had silenced the disciples' tongues by crucifying Jesus. How terribly disappointed and badly frightened they must have been as they listened to the apostles telling the story of Jesus in every language under the sun, and to people of so many different countries!

The strangers in Jerusalem were glad to hear what the apostles had to tell them. When night came, instead of a few faithful apostles praying together on a housetop, there were thousands of people who had heard the story of Christ and His wonderful works.

For a time, the people stayed with the disciples but soon all of them were bursting with the good news. Apostles, disciples, and strangers were hurrying to different lands carrying with them the glad tidings Jesus had brought them.

LYING AND LOSING

Harriet was going to give away her little gray dress. She had grown so big the past year that the gray dress was now a tight squeeze for her. She held it up to the light and lovingly fingered its rows of rainbow braid. She admired that rainbow braid and the gray buttons splashed with gay colors. "Why should I give away the braid and buttons?" Harriet asked herself. And then added, "Mother can use them on another dress for me."

She shrugged her small shoulders as she thought, "I promised my Sunday-school teacher I would give her a whole dress for the Christmas box she is sending to the girls' orphan asylum. Well, it will be a whole dress even without the braid and buttons. Besides, braid and buttons never kept anyone warm."

So down she sat and with sharp scissors slashed away at the rainbow braid. What did it matter if her clumsy fingers sometimes made a hole in the soft wool of the dress? Snip, snip, off came the buttons. "The little girl who gets this dress can fasten the back with pins," thought Harriet.

The next day a dozen small girls brought their Christmas offerings to their teacher for the box she

BARNABAS BRINGS PETER A BIG BAG FULL OF MONEY

was to send away. A pretty kimono was held up for them all to admire. A soft, warm sweater and wool cap to match were packed away in the box. Then some handkerchiefs on whose borders danced gay-colored butterflies went in. Harriet grew uneasy as she noticed that everything laid away in that box had all its buttons and trimming on.

The teacher held up a dress, an unsightly object. In the gray skirt were ugly holes where the braid had been torn or cut away. The back was buttonless, and the pretty collar snipped with the scissors which had slipped when Harriet had removed the top button.

ANANIAS, HIDING BEHIND A ROCK, EMPTIES HALF OF THE MONEY IN THE POUCH OF HIS BELT

"Whose dress is this?" asked the teacher.

"Mine," answered Harriet. "It is too small for me, so I'm giving it away to some poor little girl."

"But Harriet, all of the dress is not here," said the teacher.

"Yes, it is," replied Harriet, but she hung her head, ashamed to meet the eyes of her teacher or her classmates.

"Harriet, no one asked you for your dress, but you offered to give the box a dress, one that some poor little girl would be happy to wear. This dress is not fit to wear. It is not whole. You have ruined it with your scissors."

Many people, big and little, act Bible stories without knowing it. Harriet did.

Suppose you and I pay another make-believe visit to Palestine. What do you suppose we shall see this time? A great group of happy-looking people crowding around Peter and the other apostles. We shall see a man named Barnabas pushing his way through the crowd. At last he reaches Peter and hands him a big bag full of money.

"I sold my rich fields this morning," I can hear Barnabas say. "Here is all the money that they brought. Take it and use it for those in our company who are in need."

More people are coming, each one bringing something to the apostles.

"We don't want to own anything ourselves, we wish to share all we have with others," they said.

Who were those "others" that these generous people were talking about? Everyone who believed in Jesus and was called "Christian." In the days of the apostles not a single Christian ever went hungry, cold, or friendless.

Look! There comes a man who doesn't seem a bit happy. What can the matter be? Perhaps his feet hurt him, for he hesitates so when he walks. He has a big bag with some money in it. It doesn't look fat like the other bags given to Peter. It is lank and lean, as though it were hungry and wanted more to fill it. Ah, I know! That man hid behind a rock and emptied half the money into a pouch concealed in his belt. At last he reaches Peter and throws the half-filled bag at his feet. I don't think Peter is pleased.

"There is the price of my farm," said Ananias, the man with the lean bag.

I can see Peter's look of surprise as he lifts the lean bag. Then I know he said to the man, "Your great farm so rich and filled with fine cattle was sold for this small sum!" He must have shaken his head as he looked squarely into the eyes of Ananias, adding, "You have kept back part of the price."

Can you hear Ananias answering almost in a whisper? "The money in the bag is all I got for it."

I can see Peter look sorrowfully at Ananias as he hands back the bag. Everyone in that company knew Ananias had not told the truth. His land was valuable and he must have sold it for a large sum. And I believe everyone in that company knew that Ananias never would have sold it unless he had received a big sum for it.

"YOU ARE TRYING TO CHEAT GOD," PETER SAID

"No one asked you to sell your farm, neither have we asked for the money you received for it," replied Peter. "By keeping back part of the price, you are trying to cheat God, not us. You have lied to God, not to men."

Ananias, white with terror, gazed with frightened eyes at the apostles and the crowd around them. "Lied to God," Peter had said. Those awful words thundered in his ears. He could feel his heart knocking against his side. He had deceived no one but himself. Ananias had brought an offering in God's name and had lied when he gave it. Peter would not take it. God,

121

FEAR STOPPED THE BEATING OF ANANIAS' HEART AND
HE DROPPED AT THE FEET OF THE APOSTLES

ONE OF THE SEVEN

Philip had been turned out of Jerusalem. Scribes and Pharisees were determined that he should not teach any more people about Jesus. The apostles were sorry to lose Philip because he was such a help to them. He with six other good men looked after the poor widows and little children who called themselves Christians, and kept them from starving.

The Christians were dreadfully abused. Many of them were turned out of their homes and had to live in caves. Sometimes they had to hide in the tombs among the rocks.

whose word is truth, of course would not accept it. Not another word was Ananias able to utter. His tongue, dry and stiff with fear, refused to move. "You have lied to God!" Again those words rang through his mind. Lying to save something, he had lost everything. His fear stopped the beating of his heart and he dropped down at the apostles' feet — dead.

Ananias had sold his property for the benefit of others, but greedily kept back part of the price. Did Harriet do any better when by cutting off its braid and buttons she ruined the pretty gray dress she was giving away?

SOMETIMES THE PERSECUTED CHRISTIANS HAD TO
LIVE IN CAVES

They were stoned, whipped, burned, and even thrown to savage lions to be torn in pieces. But for some reason which their enemies could not understand, the more the Christians were abused the larger and more powerful grew the company of people who followed the apostles.

"Why can't we keep them still?" asked ruler, priest, and Pharisee.

"Nothing frightens them," said a scribe.

"What are we going to do about it? Soon the whole world will be running after them and become Christians," said all of them.

Because the rich rulers hated everyone who spoke of Jesus, they had driven Philip out of Jerusalem. Foolish rulers, how little good sense they had! By making Philip leave the city they only gave him a splendid opportunity to tell the story of Jesus and his works to many other cities and to a great many more people.

Philip's eyes were always busily watching. No matter where he was, his eyes were sure to discover someone he could talk to about Jesus. One day when he was walking in the wilderness near Jerusalem, Philip saw a handsome chariot drawn by beautiful horses standing by the roadside. A man was sitting in the

BESIDE THE ROAD PHILIP SAW A MAN SITTING IN A CHARIOT BUSILY ENGAGED IN READING

chariot reading. "How strange to stop his horses and begin to read out here in the hot sun!" Philip must have thought. When he studied he usually went up on the roof and sat in the shade.

He moved closer to the chariot. The man who was reading had a puzzled look on his face. "Surely something must be troubling him greatly. I wonder if I can help him?" thought Philip. The man began to read aloud.

"Do you understand what you are reading?" asked Philip politely.

"I do not," answered the man. "Can you help me?"

Philip climbed into the chariot and looked over the man's shoulder. "Why, that is a chapter from our Scripture!" he exclaimed. "This man must love the writings which tell about God. He will surely want to hear about Jesus." So Philip told the story as the man chirruped to his horses and the chariot rolled along on its journey to Ethiopia, where the man lived.

The man was very, very rich. He was a member of the queen's household and a powerful leader. Many, many people obeyed his commands.

"You must baptize me," said the man to Philip, "for I want to be a Christian."

Philip's heart must have sung for joy. His enemies in Jerusalem no doubt were rubbing their hands in glee, thinking that Philip was unhappily wandering among the tombs afraid to speak again of Jesus. They would probably have opened wide their eyes, and gnashed their teeth with rage, could they have seen that magnificent chariot rapidly carrying the powerful Ethiopian ruler toward his home. Soon his great country and its people would hear the wonderful message Philip had brought him about Jesus. His enemies had made this possible by driving Philip the preacher out of Jerusalem.

THE GREAT MISSIONARY

Let us watch another procession. This is not a long one. It is only a few people traveling together on their donkeys. There they go, a line of them picking their way along the road from Jerusalem to Damascus. All of them seem to be in a great hurry, especially one man who as he goes angrily shoves some letters into the pocket of his mantle. This man is Paul. He has asked the high priest to permit him to go to Damascus to arrest every person who believes that Jesus taught people the truth. When he started on his errand Paul really felt very savage about the matter. While in Jerusalem Paul had beaten the "People of the Way," as the Christians were first called, and had even ordered some of them to be put to death.

A dreadful thing happened just before Paul started to Damascus. He saw a howling mob of cruel men drag the disciple Stephen through the streets and stone him to death outside the city. Paul did not try to stop their wickedness. He even helped the men by holding their long, flowing mantles while they threw the stones. Paul intended to destroy every person

PAUL, BLINDED BY THE WONDERFUL LIGHT, BEING LED TO DAMASCUS BY HIS COMPANIONS

OFTEN PEOPLE WHO FOLLOWED THE TEACHINGS
OF JESUS WERE PUT IN CHAINS

we can't catch these people in the synagogue we will drag them out of their houses," said Paul.

He heard the hoofs of his donkey pattering on the ground. An eagle screamed above him, and the hoarse call of a vulture made him shiver. It was noon, the sun was bright. Why should Paul shiver? Surely he could not feel cold in the hot sun! I believe I know what he was thinking about, and it made him half ashamed of his errand. He must have been thinking of Stephen and saying to himself, "That man Stephen felt kindly even toward the men who abused him, while I am cursing people who never did me any harm, and swearing to injure them." Do you suppose that if Paul compared himself with Stephen it made him ashamed of himself? I think it did.

Suddenly Paul put his hands before his eyes. A light brighter than the noonday sun shone around him. It blinded him and he fell to the ground. Then he heard a voice saying, "Why do you persecute me?"

And Paul cried out, "Who are you, Lord?"

"I am Jesus," was the reply.

Paul arose. The light had been so bright that it made the daylight

who spoke the name of Jesus. If he found any people in Damascus who followed Jesus, he expected to put chains on them and bring them back with him to Jerusalem. Men and women, and perhaps even children, he would put in prison.

How brave Paul felt as he and his friends rode through the country to Damascus! How straight he must have sat upon his donkey! He whipped the little animal into a gallop, so anxious was he to reach Damascus! "Hurry, hurry, we have no time to lose," I can almost hear Paul call to his men. He must have been far ahead of them, for Paul never hung back when he had anything to do. "If

seem like darkness. He could not see, and his companions were so astonished they could not speak. They led Paul the rest of the way to Damascus.

Paul was changed. In the vision Jesus had told him that he was to be an apostle to the Gentiles. All people must be taught that God loves everybody. Jesus was a Jew, but his religion was for every kind of people under the sun. Paul was to carry this good news into every country. Not one of the disciples was able to do this work as well as Paul did it. The disciples believed Jesus came to be king of the Jews. But after Paul had talked with Jesus on the way to Damascus, he saw that Jesus came to help all people. I believe the words of Stephen when he prayed for his enemies helped Paul to see that Jesus was more than king of the Jews. He realized that Christ came to be Lord of the whole earth, because He taught that love was for all people.

Paul was quick about everything. No one ever had to wait for him. I am sure when something had to be done he never said to anyone, "Just wait a minute." That was one of the reasons he made such a good apostle.

The great hate in Paul changed to great love after his talk with Jesus

in the vision. And Paul wasn't afraid of anything. People whose hearts are filled with love forget how to be afraid.

A few days after Paul reached Damascus his sight was restored. Then he walked into the synagogue and began to tell people that Jesus was Christ, the Son of God.

Until Paul was an old man he sailed over seas and traveled through many strange countries, healing the sick and preaching the good news that God is love, and that Jesus is His beloved Son. While Paul did not know it, he was Christ's first missionary in far away lands carrying the gospel to the whole world.

PAUL WENT ABOUT PREACHING THE GOSPEL AND HEALING THE SICK

A STRANGE TABLE

How many of you little folks have dreams? All of you, I know. Some dream at night when they are asleep, while others dream in the daytime, awake, with their eyes wide open. Most dreams are foolish, but once in a while a dream tells us something important, something that we should really remember. Big folks and little folks have strange dreams. The apostle Peter had one, and it was so very odd that I must tell you about it.

And when do you think the dream came to him? At noonday when the sun was at its brightest. This was the way the dream came about. Peter was very hungry. He lived in a house by the seashore, and as salt breezes give one a big appetite, it's not surprising that by noontime he was as hungry as girls and boys who come trooping home from school in a hurry for their dinner.

When Peter was so hungry, and dinner was not yet ready for him, what do you think he did? He went up on the housetop. Surely a hungry man could find nothing to eat on the roof. But in Palestine, where people live so differently from us, they do things that seem queer to you and me. Many of the houses have flat roofs. People sometimes set up little tents on them where they can keep cool in the daytime and sleep comfortably at night. Peter wanted to pray, so he went to the housetop where he could be alone and quiet.

While Peter was praying a strange thing happened. He thought he saw the heavens above him open and a great vessel like a sheet gathered up at the four corners come slowly down to him until it rested upon the roof. Perhaps he rubbed his eyes or pinched himself to make sure he was awake. He was wide awake when the dream, or vision, came to him. Was he frightened? Not a bit, only very greatly surprised. If the sheet had been empty, perhaps he would then have turned away and gone downstairs to see if dinner was now ready. But it was not empty. And here is the odd part of the story. The sheet was full of animals. All kinds of beasts and birds and creeping things were in it, but not a single fish. "Not a fish!" Peter must have thought. "And I am a fisherman. and used to eating fish."

Here was plenty of meat waiting to be killed and eaten. He need not go hungry. But Peter did not move. He only looked with surprise and displeasure at the big sheet filled with animals.

A WONDERFUL VISION OR DREAM CAME TO PETER AS HE WAS ALONE ON THE HOUSETOP PRAYING

"Rise, Peter, here is food for you. Kill and eat," said a Voice.

"I cannot," replied the apostle. "The sheet is full of unclean animals that are not fit to eat. I never touch anything that is unclean."

"God made these animals. They are His works. What right have you to say that something God has made is unfit to eat or touch?"

Peter listened to the Voice which spoke to him, but still he would not touch the animals in the sheet let down before him. Three times this strange vessel, or sheet, filled with animals was drawn up to heaven and as many times let down

before Peter. Each time the Voice begged him to eat, but Peter turned away saying, "I never eat anything unclean."

If Peter was foolish about eating he was wise as to one thing: He began to think about this dream. "What can it mean?" I can hear Peter say as he came slowly down from the roof.

Three men were waiting for him below. All day and all night they had traveled to find him. "Does Simon, called Peter, live here?" the men asked the doorkeeper.

"I am Peter," answered the apostle when he saw the men waiting at the door. Then I am sure he thought to himself, "What can these people who are Gentiles want with me who am a Jew? Gentiles are heathen, and are common and unclean. We Jews do not associate with them."

"Will you come home with us?" the men asked Peter.

"Why do you ask me?" replied Peter. "You know that we Jews never have anything to do with the heathen."

"We wish to know about the truths you teach," replied the men. "Cornelius, our master, has sent for you. He and all his household wish to learn about the true God."

NOW PETER KNOWS THE MEANING OF HIS DREAM

Now Peter knew the meaning of that strange dream, or vision, upon the housetop. God loves every one of His children. To Him each girl or boy, man or woman, is a treasure to be treated with respect and loving kindness.

"I cannot call any people common and unclean," thought Peter to himself, "for I know God made them all."

The men stood waiting at the door. Very likely Peter stretched forth both his hands in a cordial welcome and said, "I shall be glad to go with you, for the message I can bring to you is for all people."

THE GENTILES WISHING TO LEARN ABOUT GOD ARE ASKING PETER TO GO HOME WITH THEM

PRISON DOORS

Peter was in prison. He must have been very uncomfortable, for his hands and feet were bound with chains and he was sleeping between two soldiers. What had he done? Nothing, except to tell the people the story of Jesus. And the people were so glad to hear it that many of them stopped listening to the scribes and Pharisees and would not give any more money to the synagogues. Instead, they hid in caves and in secret rooms where they could feel safe while they listened to Peter and the other apostles as they told them about Jesus.

Every day more and more people came to hear Peter. The new church that told about Jesus was rapidly growing so large that scribes and Pharisees, priests and rulers were frightened. "What shall we do to stop their talking?" they had asked each other as they saw the crowds following Peter and the apostles. "Perhaps King Herod will help us," said the rulers and Pharisees among themselves.

"If it pleases you I will stop their telling that story of Jesus," Herod said to the Jews who hated the apostles. So Herod killed James and put Peter in prison. But Herod's cruelty didn't help the Jews

PETER ASLEEP ON THE COLD STONE FLOOR OF THE PRISON

who hated the followers of Jesus and the new church called Christian. They probably expected to see the people running back to the synagogue to ask the rulers not to kill them because they had listened to Peter. But the rulers were disappointed. And how they must have scowled as they saw some rich disciples carrying gold and silver money in their bags to give to Peter for the new church!

Let us watch Peter as he lies asleep on the cold stone floor of the prison. His jailers no doubt were wishing Herod would kill Peter so they could go back to their warm, light homes. I know Peter must have smiled in his sleep, for he knew

THE CHAINS FELL FROM PETER'S HANDS AND FEET

every member of the new church was awake and praying for him. And their prayers were heard and answered. How? Watch!

Suddenly the dark, damp prison grew brilliantly light. Some one standing beside Peter tells him to wake up. Peter, astonished, opened his eyes and stared. "Am I awake or dreaming?" he asked himself.

"Rise quickly," the shining figure said, and added, "Fasten your sandals and put on your cloak."

Peter obeyed. The chains fell from his hands and feet as though they had rotted with rust. "It must be a vision," Peter thought. "Surely no one is strong enough to pass all the prison guards and come to help me." The light which awakened Peter had put his two jailers to sleep.

"Come with me," said the friend that Peter called an angel.

Past the first and second guards went Peter and his shining guide. No one noticed them. Did the light that guided Peter make blind the soldiers who guarded the prison? I think so. On the two walked. The heavy iron gate of the prison opened noiselessly of itself to let Peter and his guide pass through. Then it as quietly closed. But Peter and his guide were free and walking in the city street.

When Peter turned to thank the one who had led him out of the prison, the shining figure was gone. He was alone, and no light was near but some dim torches carried by watchmen. "Now I know my visitor was a messenger of God sent to save me from Herod," thought Peter.

He was saved just in time, for when morning came Herod had decided to put Peter to death as he had James.

Softly Peter glided through the streets of Jerusalem. At last he reached a friend's house. Rap! rap! What a noise his knuckles must have made as they beat upon the door! Were his friends glad to see him? Surely. But do you know that at first his friends would not believe it

PETER'S FRIENDS THINK THEY SEE A VISION

was Peter standing in the doorway? They thought they saw a vision.

"Tell all the disciples that I have escaped. Their prayers for me have been answered," Peter said to his friends. But he could not stay with them, for he knew when morning came Herod would send his soldiers after him. So out Peter went into the darkness and found a place where he was safe from the cruelty and hatred of ruler and Pharisee.

Did Peter stop talking about Jesus after his escape from prison? Never! He talked all the more. Once he had kept still because he was afraid. Now the apostle who once had denied that he knew Jesus, became the first to declare His name.

SHIPWRECKED

A group of angry men were standing in front of the synagogue. Priest and Pharisee, scribe and ruler were shaking their fists and sometimes shrieking aloud in rage.

"We must stop this man Paul from preaching," hissed a Pharisee.

"Only ignorant people and the poor listen to the preaching fishermen who were Jesus' apostles," declared a scribe.

"But everyone listens to Paul. He is educated and is a Roman citizen," added a high priest.

"Why, would you believe it, even the king asked Paul the other day to tell him about Jesus!"

PAUL STANDING BEFORE THE KING TELLING HIM
ABOUT JESUS AND HIS WORKS

The ruler who spoke the last words clenched his fist as he spoke. He, with the others, was afraid so many people would be running to hear Paul that no one would be left to go to the synagogue.

"Let us send him away from our country or kill him," they all said.

Paul was having a hard time of it. Ever since that ride to Damascus when he had met and talked to Jesus in a vision, the Jews had sought to kill him. Once they had trusted him as their friend. Now they thought him an enemy and really were afraid of him. Even the apostles at first didn't believe he was honestly their friend and meant what he said when he talked about Jesus.

"How can this man who once imprisoned the Christians and put many of them to death, now preach Jesus?" many of the apostles had asked.

But nothing discouraged Paul. He went right on preaching and traveling all over the country. Everywhere he went he left behind him a little company of people who believed in Jesus and practiced His teachings. Soon the whole world would hear about Jesus if Paul were allowed to speak. And this was what scribe and Pharisee, priest and ruler feared.

The apostles and other disciples at last believed that Paul was in earnest, and they welcomed him as an apostle of Christ. He could do more than any of them because he could reach more people.

The Jews who would not listen, had Paul arrested and brought before the king. "Kill him," they demanded. The king shook his head.

"What have you done?" asked the king of Paul.

"Nothing," answered Paul, "but I wish to go to Italy and talk to the emperor. I will let him decide whether I am right or wrong in preaching Jesus."

So off he started. But how do you suppose he went? In a ship, of course, but not as you or I would go. We would be free, able to walk about the decks and enjoy ourselves. Paul could not do so, for he went as a prisoner, guarded by Roman soldiers.

The ship sailed and sailed. It looked as though it never would reach Italy, the sea was so rough and the winds were so fierce. Great waves towered high above the ship and swept over it, but the sturdy little ship shook them off and sailed on. Black clouds gathered in the sky and blotted out the sun by day and the stars

"LET US SAVE OURSELVES," SAID THE SAILORS, AS ONE BY ONE THEY HURLED THEMSELVES INTO THE ANGRY WAVES

by night. Huge waves driven by the fierce winds lashed the ship's sides as though they wanted to send it to the bottom.

"Do not go any farther," said Paul, "the voyage is too dangerous. You may lose your ship and all its freight."

But the captain would not listen to him. He was in a hurry to get to Italy for the winter. Far, far away from the sheltering shore sailed the ship. Boom! Swish! Crash! Wind and wave nearly tore the brave little boat to pieces. The captain had sailed right into the teeth of a mighty storm, and the vessel was like a tiny shell crushed between its jaws. The boat was helpless. So were the passengers, and also badly frightened.

"We are lost!" all of them cried.

"Not so," said Paul. "Your ship and its freight will be lost, but every man on board will be saved. Last night in a vision God told me so."

"Let us throw over an anchor," said one of the sailors. This was done, then up it was drawn. Down again into the sea it was cast, but not so far did it sink, for the ship was nearing land.

"Put off the lifeboat and let us save ourselves," said the sailors.

"If they leave the ship without us you cannot be saved," declared Paul to the chief captain.

"We will kill the prisoners lest they try to escape," answered the soldiers.

"The prisoners shall not be killed, they shall go with us," said the chief captain. He knew Paul and loved him. He was not going to allow any harm to come to him.

The ship was slowly breaking to pieces as the waves beat against it. All the freight had been thrown into the sea to allow the ship to float.

Then a sailor cried out, "See, the lifeboat has drifted away! Now

PAUL BUILDING A FIRE FOR THE SHIPWRECKED MEN

we will have to swim if we want to reach the shore!"

"Be quick, jump overboard, every-one that can swim, and make for the shore!" shouted soldier and ship captain. "The others must try for the shore on boards or broken pieces of the ship."

The morning fog like a gray blanket hung over the sea and the sinking ship. Away in the distance could be seen a faint shore line. All were asking themselves whether the men could make it before their strength left them. One by one the men hurled themselves into the angry waves. It was a long swim, but Paul and every one of them came safely to shore. Dripping and shivering they thankfully stepped upon land once more. Paul built a fire for them. Not a prisoner tried to run away.

Did Paul get to Rome? He surely did, and for two years there in his own house he told the story of Jesus. Paul's enemies had not closed his mouth as they had hoped. Instead they had helped him to carry his message to other countries and to many people. Storm and tempest and angry sea could not stop his tongue. Never was his tongue silenced until it had told to all the civilized world the story of its King, the Christ.

THE CITY OF THE GREAT KING

Astonished, I looked out over the lake. Only a few minutes before I had seen nothing but water. But now! I took off my glasses and rubbed my eyes, to see what ailed them. Not a thing was the matter with them, and yet I was very sure my eyes were not telling me true stories. Why? Because coming out of the water and resting on the blue waves I could see a city with streets and houses. People and carts were moving along the roads. "Oh, a mirage!" I said to myself as the city slowly faded away and nothing was to be seen but the blue waters of the lake. While it lasted the mirage looked like a real city. Some people see things with their minds instead of their eyes, and call them visions. I have always thought a vision was something like a mirage. We really do see what we are looking at, even though it isn't there.

In the country of Palestine, where it was so hard for poor people to live, because no one tried to make them happy, some very dreadful things happened. Here wicked rulers and bad priests were trying to kill the people who loved Jesus. Some were burned to death, and many were fed to hungry lions and

POOR AND HOMELESS PEOPLE IN PALESTINE

tigers. Even babies whose fathers and mothers loved Christ were killed.

John, one of the apostles, was not a bit frightened by these cruel deeds. He felt sure that some time all the world would be Christian. On the little island of Patmos, in the sea far west of Palestine, John had a wonderful vision. He saw a new heaven and a new earth where everything was just as God wanted it to be.

Suppose you and I have another walk together. Let us try to see things as they ought to be. My first picture is a sad one. It is a hot summer day. The city streets are dusty and crowded with people. Flies crawl over the rubbish heaps piled high near the sidewalks. Little sick babies are crying for milk which their mothers cannot buy.

Like a mirage the picture fades and another takes its place. It is the same city, but the streets are wide and clean. On both sides of the street the pretty white houses in their new coats of paint, look as if they were smiling. There are no ash heaps or rubbish anywhere. Are there any sick children? Yes, in that big brick building. Let us go softly up the steps and peep into a room. Many small beds are in it, each one so clean that it looks like a snowdrift. Sick babies are being rocked, fed, and cared for by kind nurses.

What can have happened to make such a change in a city? I know. Some of Christ's love has come into the hearts of the people. Wherever His love goes, old and wicked places are made over into new and good ones. Hungry boys and girls, ragged and dirty, become clean and sweet, and sit down to tables covered with good things to eat. People with the love of Jesus in their hearts are always hunting for lonesome folks so that they can make them happy. No one is sobbing or crying, for selfishness and everything else that is wicked have gone away to stay.

Do you wonder that when the apostle saw how beautiful the world would be when Christ ruled, he said it was like a new Jerusalem— a new city that seemed to come down from heaven? Perhaps at the very time he saw the vision of that heavenly city, he may have heard the shrieks and screams of angry people stoning Christians in the streets of the old city of Jerusalem. I like to feel that he knew there was sure to be a new Jerusalem. Wicked things never last. You and I believe that everything really good comes to stay with us. And that is what John knew and saw and that is what he told us.

In "The City of the Great King," the New Jerusalem, all the people are kind because their hearts are filled with love. There no one can lose anything or be sick or die. And, best of all, in that city no one will ever be afraid. That is the kind of city God makes.

Do you know we can help build "The City of the Great King" by being kind, by helping everyone who needs us? I must tell you the name of the city. No, you needn't hold up your hands. It isn't the city built with bricks and mortar you are thinking about. "The City of the Great King" is not built like any other city. Its stones are all loving deeds, and its name is Christianity.

FAR AWAY FROM PALESTINE ON THE LITTLE ISLAND OF PATMOS IN THE SEA, JOHN HAD A WONDERFUL VISION.
HE SAW A NEW HEAVEN AND A NEW EARTH

A LITTLE CHILD'S HYMN

Thou that once, on mother's knee,
Wert a little one like me,
When I wake or go to bed,
Lay Thy hands about my head;
Let me feel Thee very near;
Jesus Christ, our Saviour dear.

Be beside me in the light,
Close by me through all the night;
Make me gentle, kind, and true,
Do what mother bids me do;
Help and cheer me when I fret,
And forgive when I forget.

Once wert Thou in cradle laid,
Baby bright in manger-shade,
With the oxen and the cows,
And the lambs outside the house:
Now Thou art above the sky;
Canst Thou hear a baby cry?

Thou art nearer when we pray,
Since Thou art so far away;
Thou my little hymn wilt hear,
Jesus Christ, our Saviour dear,
Thou that once, on mother's knee,
Wert a little one like me.

—Francis Turner Palgrave

WESLEY'S HYMN

Loving Jesus, meek and mild,
Look upon a little child!
Make me gentle as Thou art,
Come and live within my heart.

Take my childish hand in Thine,
Guide these little feet of mine.
So shall all my happy days
Sing their pleasant song of praise;
And the world shall always see
Christ, the holy Child, in me!

—Abridged

TWENTY-THIRD PSALM

The God of love my Shepherd is,
  And He that doth me feed,
While He is mine, and I am His,
  What can I want or need?
He leads me to the tender grass,
  Where I both feed and rest;
Then to the streams that gently pass:
  In both I have the best.
Or if I stray, He doth convert,
  And bring my mind in frame;
And all this not for my desert,
  But for His holy name.
Yea, in Death's shady black abode
  Well may I walk, not fear;
For Thou art with me, and Thy rod
  To guide, Thy staff to bear.
Nay, Thou dost make me sit and dine
  Ev'n in my enemies' sight;
My head with oil, my cup with wine
  Runs over day and night.
Surely Thy sweet and wondrous love
  Shall measure all my days;
And as it never shall remove,
  So neither shall my praise.

—George Herbert

FIRST CHRISTMAS SONG

In the fields with their flocks abiding,
  They lay on the dewy ground,
And glimmering under the starlight
  The sheep lay white around.
When the light of the Lord streamed
    o'er them,
  And lo! from the heavens above
An angel leaned from the glory,
  And sang his song of love.
He sang that first sweet Christmas
  The song that shall never cease—
Glory to God in the highest,
  On earth good will and peace.

—An old Carol

Download
Dover Clip Art at
DoverPictura.com

- Search or browse thousands of unique, high-quality images
- Download at an incredible value
- Build a collection accessible from any device

Try it today — Don't Wait. Create!
DoverPictura.com